Marquita L. Scott

~

The Ballroom

The Ballroom is a work of fiction. The names, characters, places and incidents are the product of the author's imagination and are not true to life. Any likeness of events and persons, dead or alive are coincidental.

Copyright © 2007 by Marquita L. Scott
All rights reserved.

Published by Spread Your Wings Publishing LLC
P.O. Box 19521
Detroit, MI 48219

Cover Design by Ubangi Graphics

Printed in the United States of America
ISBN –13: 978-0-9792080-0-3
ISBN–10: 0-9792080-0-9

The Ballroom is dedicated to:
Mallori Nicole Dew, my gem

Acknowledgments

Arletha L. Hunter, Mother
Thank you for encouraging me to spread my wings. I am ready to fly now.

Minister S.L. Woody, Transforming Life Ministries
Thank you for your tireless efforts supporting me.

Erica N. Martin, Second Time Media
Thank you for keeping me on track. Your expertise and recommendations were most helpful. I'll never forget what I've learned from you.

Darlene House, House of Communications
Thank you for taking on The Ballroom project. I truly appreciate all the work you put into helping this dream come true.

Eric D. Scheible, Frasco Caponigro Wineman & Scheible, PLLC
I appreciate your personal and legal advice.

Special Thank You
Al McClinton (Upscale Dance Productions)
Officer Dew (Detroit Police Department)
Nichelle L. Hunter (Personal Trainer)
Michelle D. Johnson (My assistant, my friend)
Upscale Dance Productions

Placing his hand on the small of her back, he pushed her out and led her into the basic walk before leading her into a few half turns. And back to the basic walk, he twirled her around as she spun on the ball of her foot. They faced each other, he moved them a few paces left, spun her the other way, few paces to the right, and spun her the opposite way. He placed her hand on his shoulder then walked around her while she gracefully turned.

Jeff spun her again, few paces forward. Centering himself behind her, he gently pushed her arms out and in as she rested the back of her head in the groove of his shoulder. Her right leg stretched out and back, left leg stretched out and back. One rhythmic ride of the hips, then the entire movement a few more times. He pulled her hands tightly at her sides. Right leg forward and step, step, step, step, step. He loosened his grip, cha-cha cha step. Gently pushing her waist, she pivoted from left to right to left to right.

His arm sweeping over her head, she faced him again. He pushed her out, raised her arm and he ducked under. Raised her arm again, she ducked under his outstretched arm. Hand in hand, they walked in a circle, cha-cha cha step. Cha-cha cha step, walked in a circle and walked it out. Jeff turned her so that they were back where they started, dancing the two-step.

Jeff stood in front of her, "I'm asking you to be my partner."

He let her go and she sat in the chair, catching her breath taken by Jeff's prance. The perfect contest, the perfect partner, the terrible accident the ugly scar, the frozen dream.

Chapter One

Brooke Carrington felt blood pumping through her veins as the police cruiser she was riding in raced down the street, siren blaring, shades of red and blue filling up the darkening skies. She could feel her adrenaline increasing by the second. Brooke touched her service revolver, her club, spray and flashlight. She straightened her badge and her hat, before grabbing her pad and pen. Perspiration trickled under an armpit, she made sure her bulletproof vest was intact.

The cruiser swerved. Her partner, Officer Winston Kelley III, sounded the horn, swore and slammed his fist on the steering wheel. Brooke's head jerked up and noticed several cars quickly veering to the right. *Didn't they hear the siren?*, she thought. She caught a glimpse of her partner whose lips were tightened. He loathed when pedestrians and motorists didn't abide by the rules when police were responding to a call. She had been patrolling with Officer Kelley since the former marine joined the force. That was last summer. It was almost as if she was taking him under her wing but she enjoyed working with him. He came from a family of police officers, both his father and grandfather, high in ranking were retired but instilled in him great ethics. It seemed at times that he worked for them, not wanting to disappoint either.

Brooke closed her eyes. When she was in the third grade at Fenton Elementary, a couple of uniformed officers visited her class to talk about safety. That night, over dinner, she had asked her parents all about the police. Where were they going when the blue and red lights flashed? Why do they stand in the middle of the street and tell cars where to go? Why do they have a gun? Are there any ladies who wear the uniform, too? Can she watch the police shows on television? Can she visit the police station?

Her parents explained that police officers served and protected the community. They kept it safe for citizens and sometimes that meant having to take bad guys off the streets because they had broken the law, causing harm to themselves or worse someone else. It was then she had decided that that's what she wanted to do, keep her community safe for everyone who lived there.

Brooke opened her eyes. Eight years ago she earned a bachelor's degree from Fenton University, graduated from the police academy, took an oath and had been helping her fellow officers keep Detroit safe ever since.

Officer Kelley turned off the flashers and made a sharp left onto Copper Avenue, in a middle class subdivision. They were all too familiar with Copper

Avenue; they had been on that street many times and feared that one day, they would be calling an ambulance. She took breath after breath, willing herself to calm down. She thought that if she could help it, this would be her last trip to Copper Avenue.

Officer Kelley parked the cruiser in front of the house of the woman who made the call. Brooke noticed the curtains pulled back in the picture window as they quickly got out, crossed the street and headed up the woman's walkway. Brooke saw the curtain fall back into place and she scanned her surroundings while her partner tapped the door with his flashlight. Within moments, the door opened and a woman, old enough to be their grandmother, stepped out on the porch.

Officer Kelley stuck out his chest as he spoke. "Evening ma'am, we're responding to a call."

Brooke began jotting down information as the woman spoke. "Yes, sir. I heard the woman screaming next door," she explained.

"Did you see the woman or anyone else?" Officer Kelley asked.

"No, sir. I just heard her screaming and when I looked out my window, I couldn't see a thing. I tried to look through their windows but I didn't see anybody."

"Have you heard screaming coming from that residence before?"

"Yes, sir."

"And have you called the police?"

"No, sir, but I've seen officers several times at that home."

"Okay ma'am. Why did you decide to call us this time?"

"She screams all the time, but this time - this time, it sounded like she was dying. I'm sorry."

"What is your name ma'am?"

"Wilma. Wilma Miller."

"Okay, Ms. Miller, we will investigate the matter. You heard the screams coming from next door, right?" he asked while eyeing the house.

"Yes, sir."

"Thank you. Ms. Miller, now go back inside and thanks for the call."

Brooke watched Ms. Miller go inside her house and close the door just as Ms. Miller wiped a tear falling from her eye. Brooke tucked her pad in her shirt pocket and they started for the neighbor's house. "Ms. Kent," she said as they went up to the front door.

"Yep," he said tapping the screen with his flashlight. Seconds passed, he tapped again, this time more forceful. Several more seconds had passed before the door slowly started opening. "Fifty bucks says he'll come to the door."

A woman stuck her head slightly beyond the door. There was a clump of her hair missing from one side, a gash in her forehead, a swollen eye and she was bleeding from the nose and mouth. Officer Kelley stepped back and Brooke stepped forward.

"Good evening, Ms. Kent. I'm Officer Carrington. We got a call that screams were coming from this residence."

Ms. Kent, who had begun to cry shook her head and started to close the door. Brooke placed her foot in the door. "Ma'am, my partner and I would like to come in. We can't leave until we know that you and everyone in the house are safe."

Her eyes shifted from one officer to the next. They landed on Brooke. She wiped her nose with the back of her hand. "No screams here."

"Is your boyfriend in the house?" Brooke asked, cutting to the chase; she had been through this before.

"Yeah," Ms. Kent choked.

"Where?"

"Basement," she said catching her breath.

"Is he the only other person in the house?"

Ms. Kent pulled her bottom lip in her mouth to stop the bleeding. She nodded.

"Have the two of you been drinking alcohol?"

"Not me but he's drunk."

"My partner and I need to come in and take a look. If you don't let us in, Ms. Kent, we'll have to force our way in."

After several seconds, she opened the door. Brooke stepped in first, scanning the room before instructing Ms. Kent to sit down on the sofa in the living room. "Did he beat you up?"

"Yes. Every day," she said, sinking deeper into the cushions.

Officer Kelley began searching each room, including the upstairs before he made his way to the basement.

Brooke took in a breath and sat on the edge of the sofa across from Ms. Kent. "We're going to remove your boyfriend from the home and I'm going to ask a few questions."

"I know who you are and I've been through this before," the woman said quietly.

The boyfriend yelled from the basement, Ms. Kent jumped and grabbed Brooke's hand, digging her nails into her skin. The man was yelling that he and his lady were just having a discussion and that he did not beat her.

She gently loosened Ms. Kent's grip and told her, "'Sit here." When Brooke was out of Ms. Kent's sight, she drew her handgun and made her way to the basement. Officer Kelley was cuffing him. Brooke placed her handgun back into her holster. The shirtless man, clad in blue jeans and dirty tennis shoes, had scratches on his face, neck and torso and blood smeared over an eye.

Brooke headed toward the man fiercely. She was mad at him and was going to show him the other side of the fist. She wanted him to stop hurting that woman. She despised his cowardly behavior and self-hatred. She was tired of this man and tired of being called to this residence on Copper Avenue.

Officer Kelley gave Brooke's six-foot frame a once-over. Her jaw line tightened, her temple protruding and her slanted honey brown eyes filled with fire. He gave her a warning look, it stopped her.

The man had begun to sob, stating that he was sorry, as he was led up the stairs and through the living room. He asked Ms. Kent not to press charges, then said that he was sorry and that he loved her. She looked away, buried her face in her lap and cried.

"Bring the camera," Brooke said to her partner as she looked at the man with disgust. She stood on the porch while Officer Kelley put the man in the back of the squad car. Returning into the home and sitting on the sofa, she told her, "Ms. Miller is concerned about you." Brooke paused and pulled out her pad and pen. "From the beginning," she said patiently.

The woman pressed her swollen red fingers to her eyes, the blood dried on the backs of her hands. She sighed. "I was out back watering the plants when he came home from drinking with his friends." She placed her hands in her lap, opened her eyes and wiped her running nose. "And, umm. And I uh. I could see it in his face when he got of our car. Satan had come home and he came home to get me. I uh, I uh forced a smile, then turned to finish watering the plants. He headed toward me and I didn't know what to say or if I should say anything."

Brooke placed her hand on Ms. Kent's shoulder. "Go on."

"And umm, I umm. I saw a loose brick that had fallen from the porch. I figured I could use it to hit him back if I had to. I uh pretended to be watering the plants because all the water had run out and..." She started crying again. "And he came up and I could smell the liquor. He pulled my hair and asked me why I couldn't be as hot as the women at the bar. I dropped the water pot and that's when it started. I screamed and screamed in pain as he flipped me on the very brick I was planning to hit him with, pounding on me with his fist like I was a man."

The women turned toward the opening door and saw Officer Kelley, who handed Brooke the Polaroid camera and left.

"Go on, Ms. Kent."

"I was able to get my head from off the brick, grab it and hit him in the head. He fell back and screamed and I ran toward the house to get away but he caught me inside the doorway. Soon, he grew tired of hitting me and went into the basement. Then you came to the door like you or some other lady cop does every other week."

"But you always send us away, Ms. Kent. I can't let you send me away this week. And I don't want you to die. Look at you. He could have killed you."

She squared her shoulders. "I know." Ms. Kent went on to tell Officer Carrington how they met and how a few months later, the violence started. Still, she hoped things would change after they decided to live together. Year after year he promised he'd marry her but instead of a ring she got bruises, scars, broken bones and swollen body parts, more than she cared to remember. "This is it Officer Carrington. I don't have much strength but with the little strength I have, I'm putting an end to this. I am, for once, in seven years pressing charges. No more."

Brooke wanted to smile but she did not. Instead, Brooke made sure Ms. Kent really wanted to press charges. She stood in one swift movement, took photos of Ms. Kent, told her what would happen to her boyfriend and what procedures she should follow.

For the first time, Brooke took a look around the modern, neatly kept sitting room. A sofa, a couple of winged back chairs, an end table, coffee table and plants in every corner. The bookcase was filled with books but the mirrored wall caught her attention. There was a crack in a few of the pieces of glass and there was a shoebox. One single sandal lay sideways on top of the box, which had the words, "Lady's Latin Sandal" inscribed on the side.

Ms. Kent stood with her and embraced her. "Thank you Officer Carrington, let the healing begin."

"It will Ms. Kent. You're making the right decision by choosing life." Brooke turned toward the door.

"Officer Carrington?" Ms. Kent called after her.

Brooke faced her. "Yes?"

"If you ever come down Copper Avenue again, it won't be for me."

Brooke nodded and left the residence. Officer Kelley, who had been standing outside of the cruiser, met her in the middle of the street.

"Are you all right, Carrington?"

"Yeah. Give him his charge and read him his rights."

"I saw it coming, you were going to break his face!"

"I wanted to. He's a coward and a bully." She slammed a fist into a palm. "I hate bullies."

"I wanted to break his face, too, you understand why I stopped you."

"Of course, Kelley but you know like I know it's hard to keep your emotion out of it."

He nodded.

"You keep me in place sometimes and most times I feel I'm suppose to be taking you under my wing."

"We keep each other in place. Don't sweat it. And by the way, I've learned a lot from you Carrington, you're one heck of a policewoman."

Wiping her brow, she told him, "You owe me fifty."

Brooke got in behind the wheel, Kelley on the passenger side. They drove off of Copper Avenue and for some reason Brooke believed that if she came back, it wouldn't be for Ms. Kent.

Three more hours left.

Brooke raced her own car in the driveway of her home in an upper class subdivision on the west side of the city; bringing it to a screeching halt as she self-consciously did every morning about one o'clock a.m. when she returned from her afternoon shift. She turned off the ignition and sat for a few moments, listening to the jazz station. The D.J. was advertising The Ballroom, an upscale restaurant and nightclub, opening its doors to dancers or would be dancers for Detroit Club Style Ballroom lessons. Her thoughts drifted to Ms. Kent. Closing her eyes and shaking her head, willing the very thought of Ms. Kent and any part of her job out of her head, she tuned back to the voice on the radio, missing the end of the advertisement.

Going into the house, she picked up her mail from its designated spot and noticed that an *Apartment Guide* had been included there as well. She let out a quiet giggle at the obvious hint that didn't matter. Brooke would wait for the next edition, she always did. She went into the kitchen, set the envelopes on the counter, along with the

Apartment Guide, placed her bag on the floor and washed her hands to prepare to feast on one of her mother's succulent meals. Her mother, who cooked dinner every day, left a plate on the stove, making it simple. Pulling back the aluminum foil, her meal consisted of two smothered pork chops, green beans and mashed potatoes. This is why the *Apartment Guide* had no power. She put the plate in the microwave, retrieved her mail and her bag and walked up the long winding staircase and down the hall to her parent's room. Pushing their door open slightly, she listened to their heavy breathing. She really didn't like waking them to tell them she made it in safely but they insisted. They were always concerned about her safety from her first day on the job up until the present.

When she officially announced her career choice, the Carrington household became a sad household. David Carrington, her father, at that time an attorney and now Wayne County's lead prosecutor, wanted her to go to law school. Never, had he thought his little girl would choose such a tough job, a job that was dangerous and risky. A job that would harden her, maybe even make her depressed, crazy or worse kill her. He assumed all the talk about being an officer was just that, talk. Jenna Carrington, her mother, also an attorney at that time and now a Wayne County judge, also had aspirations of her daughter sitting on the bench, if not in front of it practicing law. Her sentiments were that of her husband's. "More civilians are killed than police," Brooke had argued. "I'll be fine, just wait, you'll see. I just want to help keep order in my community," was her closing argument. They realized they were losing the case and reluctantly agreed to support her.

"Mom, Dad, I'm home," she said just above a whisper. One of them mumbled, she couldn't tell which one. She closed the door and walked up a few steps to her bedroom where she unloaded her bag and mail. Making her way back downstairs, she went into the kitchen and gave her food a few more minutes in the microwave before she ate in silence. When Brooke finished, she rinsed her plate and fork, placed it in the dishwasher and went down the hall to the sitting room to check her e-mail. Moments later, back in the kitchen, she made a pineapple martini, keeping it on ice in a couple of shakers. She returned to her bedroom, closed the door and put Dave Koz's, *At the Movies* in her CD player. She went in her bathroom and poured lavender bubble bath under warm water. Surrounding the tub with lavender-scented tea light candles, she then poured the contents from the shaker into a martini glass and set both on a tub shelf. Undressing, she tossed her clothes in the hamper and got into the tub, sinking deep in the water, turning on the jets and relaxing. She heard her personal line ring and closed her eyes.

It Might be You filled the air as Brooke realized she had dozed off, martini glass empty, jets still shooting out water. Turning off the jets, she drained the tub and stood up. Grabbing her thick, cotton lilac bath towel from the towel ring, she dried off and tied it around the length of her body. Snuffing out the candles that had nearly burned out, she cleaned the tub and went into her bedroom. Then she fed Small Blue, her Beta fish, along with Small Yellow, her snail. Grabbing the remote control to her flat screen television, she pressed power and picked up *The Choice* by Nicholas Sparks when her telephone rang yet again. She looked on the caller ID. It was Irene, her maternal grandmother, whom she was very close to, as they had a great relationship. Brooke turned off the television when she answered the telephone.

"Hi, sweetheart. I was hoping you were at home."

She sat on the edge of her king-sized bed and put the book down. "Granny, what are you doing awake so early in the morning?"

"Of course, listening to the police scanner. I was listening for your squad car number."

"Granny, you should be asleep. I've told you before to stop listening to the police scanner. Where is Grandpa?"

"He's sleeping."

"And that's what you should be doing. How are you? Is everything okay?"

"Yes of course, everything is fine. I was thinking about you and wanted to talk to you. How are you?"

"I'm great, Granny. Thanks for asking."

"Good. How are your mom and dad?"

"Doing well. What did you do today?"

"While your granddad was out golfing with friends, I was doing a little shopping."

"Oh?"

"Yeah. I went shopping for you."

Her face lit up with excitement. Usually, they went shopping together and her grandmother would always get her opinion on a nice suit or dress, saying that it was for one of the young women at church. At the end of the day, her grandmother would give it to her. "What is it, Granny? A new summer dress with matching sandals? A swimsuit for the beach? A purse, bracelet, watch?"

"A date."

"A date?" She asked, less enthused.

"Yes, a date. There's a nice young man at the Senior's Club who drops his grandfather off at all the events. I told him all about you and he wants to meet you."

"No more of your blind dates!"

"Well, why not? Besides, I haven't introduced you to anyone since four months ago."

"That's because I haven't been to any of the events since four months ago."

"Which reminds me, should I save you a seat at the steak roast this Sunday evening?"

"Granny, I appreciate your matchmaking efforts but I'm dating Kyle – for four months to be exact."

Her grandmother let out a laugh. "That big oaf you introduced us to at the–"

Brooke laughed. "Granny!"

"Granny doesn't normally say anything bad about other people's children but this guy is special. He didn't have the decency to inform you he was running late and when he showed up, it was as if he was under duress. He was more interested in that cell and Palm Pilot. And when his hands were free, he used both of them to cover his yawns.

"He barely said goodbye when he left and he climbed in his car and sped off before you got to your car door. What man does that? I didn't see anything about him that was good for you."

Brooke was still laughing.

"You know what I'm saying is true, that's why you're laughing but let's be serious for the moment. Why are you still giving that man the time of day?"

Brooke didn't answer.

"I asked you a question Brooke Carrington."

"I don't know. I guess I'm just waiting for the next ship to sail in."

"The lady in waiting?"

She was quiet for a second. "Something like that."

"Something like that? You're not getting any younger, Brooke."

"I know. I work the afternoon shift and when I come home, it's late and I just...I can't...I don't know if..."

"What happened to the Brooke who was full of life and had many things to do? What happened to those old passions that had you laughing and talking about it for hours?" She didn't wait for an answer. "Whatever happened to your love for the dance?" This time it was her grandmother's turn to hold the line. Silence continued for what seemed like minutes before she broke the silence. "Squeeze a little fun time in your schedule. You need it. And stop this settling business. I mean it, you don't have to settle."

Brooke was quiet.

"Hello?"

"Okay, Granny."

"I mean it. Get busy doing something meaningful, yet fun and tons of ships will roll in; but not while you're stretched out across your king-sized bed reading romance novels."

"Okay."

"And nothing's wrong with reading romance novels but you understand what Granny means, don't you?"

"Yes, of course."

"I love you."

"I love you, too. Kiss Grandpa for me and I'm coming over to pick up that scanner tomorrow." Brooke hung up the telephone, went to her closet and grabbed her silk lavender pajamas. While she dressed, Brooke noticed her telephone indicating messages. Remembering that someone had called her while she was bathing, Brooke retrieved her message while snickering at the conversation she had with her grandmother.

The message played, *"Hi, Brooke, it's me. How are you? I don't know why I asked, it's not like you can answer me. Anyway, I don't know what to say or actually, I don't how to say it. I don't know if I should say it over the voice mail but I better say it before I lose the nerve."* There was a pause. *"I can't see you anymore."*

Replay.

"Hi, Brooke, it's me. How are you? I don't know why I asked, it's not like you can answer me. Anyway, I don't know what to say or actually, I don't how to say it. I don't know if I should say it over the voice mail but I better say it before I lose the nerve. I can't see you anymore."

Brooke laughed until her stomach ached then she laughed some more. Typical of Kyle to leave a message on her answering machine, knowing that she was at work. She pulled the covers back, got into her bed and opened *The Choice* to chapter ten.

She read a little, thought about what her grandmother said, laughed a little, read a little more, laughed at the message on her answering machine and eventually, she sunk deep into the firm mattress and snuggled over her spring fresh scented covers and fell asleep. The laughter continued in her sleep as she dreamed about being dumped by a fool.

Brooke took note of the slightly darkened skies as she made her way inside the crowded Adorable Dough Café. Although a warm morning, rain was surely on the horizon if the overcast didn't have its way. Nonetheless, she was going to meet her dear friend, Ingrid Winter. They had made it a practice to meet for breakfast at least once a week to catch up on all the things they missed just the week before.

Five years earlier, the friends met at the Detroit Police Department's annual carnival. Ingrid and her aunt, Madison, had been personally invited by the Chief of Police, Dorian George. Madison and Chief George were college buddies and also had mutual friends. Ingrid, who had been standing in line behind Brooke at the hot dog stand, noticed her interesting, lightened hair color, complimented her and asked about it. Telling her that her curly mane had flashlights, she had given Ingrid her hairdresser's telephone number at Classic Hair Designs, one of the city's most popular hair salons. Ingrid came to the beauty shop and although she wasn't brave enough to get flashlights, she gained a better hairstylist and a friend.

Brooke spotted Ingrid at their usual corner booth by the windows skimming the *Detroit Daily* and sipping coffee. As Brooke headed her way, she couldn't help but think how amazing it was that Ingrid looked just like her aunt. She wore heavy but flawless makeup, especially over her caramel colored eyes. She kept her hair styled short, sometimes layered with curls, sometimes pulled flat and silky. This day, it was in curls. Her work wardrobe always had her in pantsuits that complimented her tall and hefty physique.

Brooke, who on her off days opted to be extremely comfortable, preferred fashionable sweats. She leaned into the booth and kissed Ingrid before sliding onto the bench across from her.

Ingrid smiled, as she began putting the newspaper back in order, "Hey Brooksey."

"Hey. Sorry I'm a little late. It felt like I had just fallen asleep when it was time for me to wake up."

"It's okay. I have a few extra minutes before I have to be at the office." Ingrid was The Winter Group's director. It was an organization offering classes for children interested in learning ceramics, papermaking, sculpting, painting and drawing.

"Sure?"

"Yep. Madison gave me a lot more flexibility since we hired Lee as the assistant director."

"Lee? The guy who used to intern at the Art Museum of Detroit with you?"

Ingrid passed her a menu that Daryl, their server, had already placed on the table. "Yep. He did such a great job Madison kept him in mind when she established The Winter Group."

"How is he working out?" she asked while opening her menu.

"Lee is doing a great job. I have no complaints at all."

Brooke stifled a yawn and said, "I remember you telling me that you were something else back then, like you just didn't have a care in the world."

"I didn't think I did have a care in the world until Madison and I started talking a lot and then I met you."

Brooke blushed.

"Really! By the time I met you, I was finally growing into adulthood, being responsible. You inspired me Brooke in so many ways, I wouldn't even know where to begin."

Brooke was about to speak when Daryl approached. "I see your lovely friend finally made it," Daryl teased as he kept his eyes on Brooke.

Brooke smiled but said evenly, "Good morning Daryl."

"Good morning, beautiful. The usual, ladies!" Daryl said to Brooke as a statement rather than a question.

Ingrid looked at Brooke who folded her menu and nodded.

"Very well. Silver dollar pancakes, a side of maple bacon and milk for Ingrid. Hash browns with cheese and onions, sausage links, toast and hot chocolate for you beautiful," he said to Brooke as if Ingrid wasn't there.

"You know us too well," Ingrid told Daryl while trying to hold her laugh.

He still kept his eyes on Brooke.

Brooke lowered her gaze to the closed menu. "Not well enough," he began responding to Ingrid's statement. "I'm really a great guy, if you'd just give me a try." He turned on his heel and walked away.

They laughed.

Ingrid finished her lukewarm coffee. "That boy is not going to give up any time soon."

Brooke shook her head. "You purposely sit in Daryl's section, don't you?"

Ingrid nodded. "I do indeed. Between Daryl's lame lines and you pretending not to notice, it's just plain funny."

"I'm glad to be able to humor you at my expense," Brooke teased. "Besides, his lines aren't that lame."

Ingrid frowned, "What?"

"I remember the first time I met Daryl. I was waiting for you and I sat at this very booth. As he walked over and caught my attention, I saw his face just light up so bright.

"He smiled and introduced himself and made small talk. And right before you came in, Daryl said when he looked up and saw me, it was like the entire room lit up."

There was silence for a moment, then Ingrid said, "Brooksey, you don't think that was lame?"

They laughed. "No I don't," Brooke continued. "I think it was sweet and sincere." Ingrid was still laughing. "Seriously, Ingrid, that was the first thing I noticed about him you know, his face lighting up and all."

Ingrid was still laughing.

"Okay, forget it. I can see that you are so not ready for the truth. This is why I get extra food and you don't."

The laughter between them continued. Daryl returned a while later with their order. Ingrid received the right amount of pancakes and bacon that came with the meal but Brooke received an extra portion of everything: a sausage link, more toast, more hash browns with extra cheese and onions, more whipped cream on her hot chocolate. Daryl lightly touched Brooke's shoulder and left.

"I got dumped yesterday," Brooke said matter-of-factly as they had begun eating.

Ingrid reached for the maple syrup. "By who?" she asked before she thought about it. "Not by that clown Kyle! You've got to be kidding me right? He's got some nerve."

She poured a little salt and pepper over her hash browns. "Left a message on my voice mail."

Ingrid swallowed a piece of bacon before she exclaimed, "Left a message on your voice mail? What a wimp. Never mind him, he did you a favor. I knew you were in trouble when that joke took you to that office party."

Brooke stifled a yawn and ate her food as she reminisced. Kyle, a stockbroker, worked for a major firm. The CEO of the firm had an office party at his lavish home in Indian Village, a very affluent community in Detroit. He invited the entire staff. Brooke was Kyle's date for the evening although it seemed as if she had attended the party alone.

Kyle had arrived at her home twenty minutes early and then became miffed because she wasn't ready. He practically hurried her out the door and into the car, not even opening or closing her doors. And the night had only gotten worse. When they arrived at the party, he hopped out of the car and started up the walk, causing Brooke to hurry out of the car, tripping over herself to fall in step with him.

Once inside, he already had his coat off and in the host's hand as another guest graciously helped Brooke with her coat. Kyle had disappeared, leaving Brooke in the foyer following the voices, listening for his and wondering which way to go. Noticing that some guests were going into the basement, she followed suit and wouldn't you know there was Kyle at the bar having a cocktail. The other stools were occupied but he didn't give up his stool for Brooke or offer her a cocktail. Kyle didn't even introduce her to the people he obviously knew.

Brooke hadn't thought it could get any worse but it did. A colleague told him that the food was being served. A while later, Kyle returned with a plate full of food for himself. Then, when lady in orange came over to greet him, he offered her his seat, told the bartender what to make for her and said he'd be back with a plate of food for her. Even lady in orange was put off after she realized Brooke was Kyle's date.

Although Ingrid herself was on a date that night, without hesitation, she and her friend picked Brooke up and took her home. Brooke hadn't even told Kyle she was leaving and that made him angry. Kyle had called the next day to say that he was embarrassed looking for his date at the end of the party and nobody knew who Brooke was or where she was. However, it was only after Brooke told him how rude and ill-mannered he was that Kyle became apologetic. Somehow he was able to convince her that there had been a misunderstanding and that she should go out with him again.

"You deserve better." Ingrid said bringing her back from her reverie.

Brooke absently blew steam from her hot chocolate and took a sip. "I know," she said. "I know."

Ingrid finished off her last pancake, "Brooke Carrington, no matter what, don't lose your focus. The one thing you hate, always hated, is mistreatment."

Ms. Kent flashed across Brooke's mind. She knew mistreatment was mistreatment and it certainly came in different forms. A good-looking man walked past their table, heading toward the men's room. "Kenneth Cole Black," Brooke said finishing her toast.

"His cologne!" Ingrid snickered.

Brooke winked at her.

"I'm rubbing off on you. Only you and I know the scent a man is wearing without him telling us. Anyway, I caught your curious stare, does this means you aren't swearing off men?"

Brooke let out a laugh. "Because of Kyle? Not a chance. I'm at peace with myself. At first, I thought that maybe Kyle would come around, too bad it took his message to end it." She pushed her empty dishes toward the middle of the table. I kind of feel like I'm back to square one but a part of me wonders if that's such a bad thing. Life is full of phases, you simply move from level to level and learn from the experiences."

Ingrid started to speak but Brooke subtly raised her hand and continued. "I won't allow myself to give up on love or give Kyle any kind of power. I'm going to push forward. I have every right to expect nothing but the best. Rejection is a part of the journey. I've come to realize and accept it."

Ingrid didn't respond at first, wanting to be sure that Brooke was finished. She placed her hand gently on top of her friend's hand, "Very well spoken. I'm proud of you and I've discovered a way for you to broaden your horizons."

Brooke pulled her hand away. "No, Granny! I mean it – absolutely no blind dates, matchmaking or anything else that may cause me discomfort."

Ingrid giggled, understanding how Brooke had felt because she too had been a member of her grandmother's dating service. Daryl returned with another cup of hot chocolate, extra whipped cream, of course for Brooke. He left another coffee for Ingrid also but he said nothing.

"On the contrary, my dear friend. Although I agree with Granny, this endeavor is really not about a man. It's really about you honing your skills, meeting new people and doing something other than working out, reading romance novels and kicking in doors."

Brooke licked her tongue out at her. Stirring her whipped cream she told Ingrid, "And anyway, you need to be at the Motor City Fitness Club with me. I keep telling you to exercise."

Ingrid flexed her arm muscle. "Look at these guns girl, I don't need a Motor City Fitness Club."

Brooke shook her head at her friend's shenanigans.

Ingrid grew serious. "I could shed a few pounds and get my heart rate up."

"So when should I sign you up? I have connections, I can get you a deal on your membership."

Ingrid playfully rolled her eyes. "Don't change the subject."

"Scary-cat."

Ingrid pushed her dishes to the middle of the table, wiped her hands on a napkin and searched through her briefcase. Pulling out a dark blue, professionally designed flier, the size of a standard invitation, she handed it to Brooke.

Brooke scanned the information detailing Detroit Club Style Ballroom lessons, "The Ballroom. I heard something about this on the radio this morning."

"Thursday night ballroom lessons throughout fall and winter with a competition in the spring. You should go."

"Why?

"I already told you."

Brooke sighed. "Are you going to take the lessons?"

"Please, you know that I've got two left feet. I can sing…" Ingrid stopped speaking and hummed a melody she had made up. "But I've seen you in action and I know that you can dance."

Brooke smiled, "That sounded beautiful."

"Think about it Brooksey, it'll be fun. Although the flier is promoting ballroom lessons, they teach other dances that may interest you."

Brooke knew that Ingrid was right and so was her grandmother. She had been dancing since she was five years old. Throughout grade school and high school she had studied dance, entered competitions and won several certificates and trophies. She even had some ballroom on her resume. The reason why she stopped dancing at all flashed across her mind but she immediately forced it from her memory. "My work shift—"

"I'll talk to Dorian when I get to the office since I know you won't go to your parents."

"You think it's that easy?"

"It is when you're Ingrid Winter."

"Brooke's taking ballroom lessons and needs to change her shift."

"Leave the influencing to me. Don't worry about how I'm going to work it out. Just tell that cutie pie Winston that the two of you will be working eight to four soon."

"We'll see Ingrid Winter." Brooke closed her eyes for a moment and opened them. "Ballroom lessons!" she pondered.

"I heard about this place and from what I hear, they say, chances are you'll fall in love at The Ballroom."

~

Chapter Two

Jeff Ryan's fingers slowly gripped the car door handle as the car he was riding in raced down the freeway. Veronica, the woman he was dating, was driving about twenty miles over the speed limit. Although it was around four thirty in the morning and the number of motorists was few, she drove inches behind cars before abruptly changing lanes only to repeat the action from one motorist to the next.

"Veronica," he said catching his breath. "Slow down."

She looked at Jeff, who was at least four inches over six feet, had extremely flawless skin, jet black curly hair and sleepy eyes, the color of silver, hiding under his extremely long lashes. Regardless the model image, she pulled her lips together, tightening her jaw line. "Slow down?" Veronica turned her attention to the road and honked her horn at someone she thought was driving too slowly.

Veronica switched lanes, glaring at the driver as she passed. "I'm trying to get you and *your friend* to the airport." She looked through her rear view mirror into the back seat at Robby, Jeff's scruffy looking childhood friend, and rolled her eyes. No one really knew what Robby looked like; he always wore baseball caps pulled low over his eyes.

"Yeah but we still have time, take off isn't until seven o'clock."

"But you have to get to the airport as early as possible to avoid long lines and to get through security."

"If we get stopped by for speeding then—"

"Jeff, you asked me to take you and *your friend* to the airport, I'm taking you so don't tell me how to drive you to the airport."

"I'm not telling you how to drive, I'm asking you to slow down, there are other passengers in the car."

She slammed on the brakes, skidding before coming to a stop. The car behind them sounded its horn and swerved into the next lane. The seat belt caught Jeff but Robby's head hit the back of her seat. "Do *you* want to drive?"

Jeff, whose hand had gripped the dashboard, willed himself to calm down. He couldn't believe she brought a moving vehicle to a halt on the freeway. *Why am I giving her the time of day?* he thought.

Veronica pressed the accelerator and continued to drive. They drove the last five minutes to Detroit Metropolitan Airport in silence. Veronica pulled up to the curve and before she could stop the car,

Robby jumped out, a brown duffle bag around his shoulder.

Jeff took a few seconds to get his bearings. "Thank you," he forced out.

Her temper cooled. "You're welcome honey." Veronica leaned over, hugged Jeff and tried to kiss him but he turned his head resulting in catching his cheek. "You're mad at me aren't you?" she asked.

Jeff opened the door and got out of the car. Pulling his leather travel bag from the back seat and gathering his matching carryon bag he told her, "I've got a plane to catch."

Jeff and Robby were standing in line to check in when Jeff noticed that Robby didn't have any luggage. He opened his mouth to ask about it but changed his mind. He felt a wave of uneasiness but forced himself to let it pass. An hour later, they checked in, received their boarding passes and went through security. They were sitting in the waiting area outside their designated gate with others flying to Cancun, Mexico. Robby had been there several times; Jeff had heard only good things about the place. The beach, good food, great drinks, lots of parties and women who hung out at them – Robby told him all of this of course and convinced Jeff to come with him for the weekend.

Although he and Robby weren't exactly living the same lifestyle, he felt some type of loyalty to his friend and could give many reasons why. When they were in kindergarten, they lived on the same block and two blocks away from school. In between their block and the school was a park, which they would walk through to get to school. One day it rained the night before and had been lightly rainy that morning. Jeff loved to walk across the baseball field and this particular morning was no exception. The "king" had forbade his two sisters, the "princesses" to get their hair wet so they ran the rest of the way, leaving the defiant Jeff and Robby behind. It wasn't long before Jeff's feet started to sink in the muddy field. He tried his best to get to safety but he could not. He started to cry, scared that he would sink. He felt his shoes and socks come off and at the same time felt Robby's arms around his waist pulling him out of the mud.

In elementary, a bully was transferred to the school. He made walking home a nightmare for all the students. Jeff and Robby knew it was a matter of time before they'd become victims. It was Jeff's plan to run home but Robby said that his dad told him if they ran home today, they would be running home every day. The day came. Robby was on detention and Jeff had to walk with his sisters and other classmates. The bully reared his ugly head, taunting and teasing Jeff, setting him up for the first blow. Jeff heard a smack and a wail followed by watching the bully fall to his knees. There stood Robby with the handle to his lunchbox in hand, half of the box on the grass, the other on the baseball diamond. Robby had handled a few other fights with the bully's friends. He'd won each one. Nobody bothered them again. Robby's father moved out that summer.

Summer months were especially fun when they were in grade school. All the children on the block, and some from the other blocks, would play in the middle of the street. They scattered as cars drove by only to gather back into the street. One day, Robby saw a car speeding down the street just as Jeff was running across. It was Robby who tackled Jeff onto the grass as the car sped by, the driver honking the horn. By middle school, Robby moved across town to live with his grandfather. Jeff's parents let him visit Robby once. And that one time an electrical wire had fallen in the backyard so Robby suggested they play catch in the driveway instead. Jeff thought he could just move the wire off the grass but it was Robby who stopped him from touching it. Robby told Jeff if he touched it he would get electrocuted and die.

Jeff and his parents moved to a neighborhood with one of the best high schools in the city while Robby attended a school for children who weren't as fortunate but they remained in contact. By the time Jeff could drive, he would visit Robby more often. Most days, they would play dodge ball with Robby's friends at the park. The park was about a seven-minute walk from Robby's house. Once Jeff tried to dodge the ball and twisted his ankle. It was Robby who carried him all the way to his car. Strapping him in the passenger seat, he fished Jeff's keys out of his pocket, got into the driver's seat and drove to the hospital.

Jeff, who was the editor for the school paper, spent a lot of time reading newspapers and rewriting some of the stories. After graduation, he entered Fenton University with a four-year scholarship to study journalism. Robby, who barely made it out of school, wasn't sure of his next move. He would spend the next ten years hopping from job to job, if even working at all. Jeff was much more serious about life. Robby didn't seem to care as long as he was making it from one day to the next.

Jeff heard his cellular phone ring. Unzipping his bag, he found it buried under *Sports Illustrated* and the *Detroit Daily*. Viewing the caller ID, he sighed. *What does she want? She just dropped us off!* He thought. Jeff hoped he didn't leave anything in her car as he answered.

"Jeff. I've got to tell you something."

"What?"

"I can't pick you and *your friend* up from the airport."

"No problem but couldn't you have told me before today so that I could've made other arrangements?"

"I suppose that would have been the best thing to do but I wasn't thinking."

"*As usual,*" he said without thinking.

"Aren't you going to ask me why?"

"It doesn't matter."

"I thought you'd never ask. You're a great guy but I can't see you anymore."

Jeff laughed.

She huffed through his earpiece. "This isn't funny, Jeff, you–"

Jeff flipped his cellular close, put it in his carryon bag and laughed some more.

Robby pulled the headphones from his iPod off his ears. "What's funny?"

He took out his MP3, turned it on and put the headphones over his ears. "I've just been dumped by a fool."

"And you're cool with Veronica breaking up with you?"

"Yep."

Putting his headphones back on, he responded, "the little engine that could."

Cancun, Mexico was beautiful from what Jeff could see as they rode in the airport van to a hotel downtown. The hotel wasn't pricey, neither was it one of the best hotels. Once they checked in, Jeff was ready to shower, change and spend some time on the beach before taking part in the nightlife. Robby had different plans. He wanted to go to the shopping center first and convinced Jeff to come with him. He agreed but took a shower first.

Once inside the mall, Robby insisted that they go separate ways and meet outside in a half hour. Jeff studied Robby, who had been tightly clutching his brown duffle bag, trying to figure out what he had up his sleeve. He opened his mouth to ask but changed his mind. Instead, he walked away from his friend, finding himself in and out of several stores before getting a good deal on a purse for his mother and a wallet for his father. Thirty minutes had passed and he met Robby outside as agreed.

Noticing a shopping bag, Jeff asked, "What did you buy?"

Robby fidgeted with his T-shirt. "Something for tonight." Looking around he said, "Let's go, come on." They walked toward the bus stop. Robby picked up his pace, Jeff on his heel. Once they came to the street, Jeff noticed the traffic guard in the bright orange vest directing traffic. Robby darted across with Jeff racing after him. Jeff heard a siren but continued to the other side of the street and hopped on one of the buses with Robby. Paying the driver six pesos, he followed Robby to the back of the bus and sat down.

Jeff saw the traffic guard run toward the bus and stop the driver. He yelled something in Spanish. Exchanging glances with Robby, Robby slid down in his seat. Jeff's heart began to pump in his chest and he began to sweat when the small police cruiser pulled alongside and then in front of the bus. The police officer got out and said something to the traffic guard, who returned to his post. He then made his way onto the bus and spoke to the driver in Spanish. The Spanish-speaking passengers gasped. The driver turned in one swift movement as the officer walked down the aisle, eyeing each passenger seat-by-seat, side-by-side.

It became extremely quiet on the crowded bus, except for the officer's shoes shuffling across the floor and sighs of the relief when he walked pass passengers. He stopped at Jeff and Robby's seat, looking Robby straight in the eyes. Jeff could feel his throat tighten. He told both of them, in broken English, to get off the bus. They did – with Jeff's legs shaking the entire time. Once off the bus, the police officer escorted them to the cruiser and demanded to look in Robby's bag. Robby explained that he paid for everything and gave the officer a receipt. The officer looked at the receipt and then at Robby, demanding he open the bag. Robby obliged, pulling out a blue T-shirt and blue jean shorts. Meanwhile, soldiers from the military crossed the street, surrounding the officer, Robby and Jeff. The officer's thick black eyebrows formed a V and he said something in Spanish. It didn't sound nice. "Shirt only," he seethed. "No shorts." He threw the shirt, shorts and receipt in the bag and said something to the military in Spanish. He ordered and at the same time escorted Robby into the police car.

Robby's eyes seemed to scream, "Save me, Jeff," as he gave his friend a once-over through the back window. The emptiness he saw in Jeff's eyes penetrated Robby's heart as if someone had stepped on it. He could never find a way to explain his trials and tribulations to the man who had never let him down.

"Wait!" Jeff yelled, bringing the officer to a stop.

He turned around and asked, "Sir?"

Jeff stared blankly at the officer as if he had forgotten what to say. Could have been fear, could have been confusion, Jeff wasn't sure.

"Sir?" The officer asked again annoyed.

Jeff swallowed then asked, "Can we speak with the store manager first? I'm sure there's a good explanation. We'd also like American representation, if that's possible," he added humbly.

The officer looked at a military police officer who fortunately spoke English and translated Jeff's question. After much dialogue in Spanish between the officer and the military police, the store manager was radioed.

"Speak to manager first. American representation when he go in." Jeff only nodded as the officer let Robby out of the police car and with two of the military police, escorted them back into the mall and into the store where Robby was accused of stealing.

In the back, on the manager's old wooden table, the officer placed the shorts, the shirt and the receipt. Jeff shook his foot nervously as he waited for the manager. Jeff could feel all eyes on him, even Robby's eyes were glued to him, but he refused to meet any of their gazes. He just kept his eyes on the evidence, hoped he could get Robby out of this or he'd be returning to the states without him.

The manager came in the small room with a frown but Jeff still relaxed a little after seeing that he was an American. However, when the manager directed his attention to the officers and spoke to them for a while in Spanish, Jeff tensed again. When he had finished, he spoke to Robby in English. "Our sales girl tells us that you didn't give her enough pesos." He placed another receipt on the table and sat down on the squeaky chair. "The shorts were five thousand, nine hundred and ninety-nine pesos which in American money is about fifty-nine dollars plus sales tax. You gave her two hundred pesos and ten dollars."

"Sir, I–"

The manager spoke over him, "She kept trying to explain that you either owed her more pesos or more dollars. She even gave you the amount and showed you on the calculator but you insisted you paid her the right amount before making your abrupt exit. Authorities were faster than you, eh?

"Now, she may not speak English well but she can count pesos, yen, euro, gelt, dolar, onza, lira, any other currency and of course, the U.S.

currency. However tourists decide to pay, she can count."

Robby sat up straight, looked directly into the manager's eyes and said, "Sir, I'm terribly sorry for all of this. I did not intentionally deceive the young lady. I thought that I had given her the right amount of money."

The room grew silent. Jeff finally looked at Robby wondering whose voice just came out of his body. And because Robby had been to Mexico several times, Jeff wondered why Robby was acting as if he didn't know about the currency exchange rates.

The manager's chair had begun to squeak as he picked up the receipt and waved it at Robby. "You intentionally left this receipt."

"No sir, I did not. I just did not think that I needed it since our transaction was final."

"You kept the other receipt!"

"She put it in my bag before I could tell her I didn't need it since our transaction was final."

The manager leaned back in his squeaky chair and glared at Robby with a smirk. "I really wish that I could prove your deception but me, nor the cameras cannot. You purchased a shirt only to return moments later with a pair of shorts, coincidence?

"I don't have time to lecture you the way I'd like so in short, I want you to understand that the people here rely heavily on tourist money for their livelihood and they deserve every penny of it. These gracious people, who work for little, also deserve your respect. If you cannot afford it, it's not for you," the manager concluded.

"Again, I'm terribly sorry." Robby said. "I wish that I could prove to you and the authorities just how sincere I am. I will pay the remaining amount for the shorts."

The manager's voice rose slightly, "You were supposed to pay for them the first time." Lowering his voice he continued, "The shirt and the shorts are now store property and will not be returned to you. And, before you leave this country, you will pay a hefty fine, which is in the thousands and if you try to skip out of town without paying it, you will need American representation."

"I'd like to apologize to the young lady for the misunderstanding."

"That's not necessary, plus, the young woman doesn't wish to speak to you."

"But, I'd really like to apologize."

"Forget it. Just pay the fine." The store manager stood up. "Depending on the rate, move the decimal point one space to the left."

"Excuse me?"

"When you convert pesos to dollars. Consider it when paying this fine."

"Thank you for the much needed advice," he retorted smugly.

The bus ride back to the hotel seemed to be a long one as no words passed between Jeff and Robby. It wasn't until they were inside their hotel room when Robby broke the ice. "How long are you going to be mad at me?"

Jeff wouldn't face him as he began packing his personal belongings. "I'm changing my plane ticket and leaving tomorrow morning."

"Over some misunderstanding? Man, get outta here."

"My how the tongue changes," he retorted sarcastically.

"What? You don't believe me?"

Jeff stopped what he was doing and met Robby's eyes. "I'll give you the money to take to the station. You can thank me later for all I've done for you. I'm out of here."

"You really don't believe me!" Robby said heading toward him.

Jeff said nothing, intensifying a long, hard, cold stare.

Robby backed off. "I don't need your money man, I'll pay the fine so you don't worry about it!"

"Where are you going to get that kind of money, Robby?"

"Where are you going to get that kind of money, Jeff?"

Jeff didn't respond.

"Right! Like I said, I don't need you to pay the fine. I'll take care of it."

Jeff faced his friend and looked at him with pity. "Then I guess I'll see you back home."

"Should I hold my breath?"

Jeff shook his head, "Grow up!"

As Robby walked out of the room, he retorted, "I'll grow up when you stop being a lollipop."

Smoke from Jeff Ryan Sr.'s Partagus Tubo cigar filled the huge, cream-colored kitchen. Glaring at his son, he fingered his salt and pepper, neatly trimmed goatee as he did when frustrated. Beside him sat, Lynne, his wife. Disappointment reflected in her silver, sleepy eyes as she sat with her arms crossed. Jeff, who was sitting across from them, was informing them about what happened in Mexico. When Jeff finished, moments had passed and it felt like he was being smothered by silence.

His mother had redecorated the kitchen once again. The chairs they were sitting on were futuristic, clear, the shape of half moons. The small table matched, set off with a vase of orange carnations. The wide, refrigerator was new, it resembled cabinetry, as did the storage areas. On the shelves were cookbooks, special dishes, pots and pans that probably won't be used. The gas stove was also new as his mother claimed she couldn't cook on an electric stove. His mother even put in a new floor with a floral pattern of mauve, to match the curtains hanging in the windows. As one of the interior designers for Homes Across Southeast Michigan, she just couldn't help but make yearly changes throughout the home. He thought for sure she would speak first but it was still quiet. His mother always spoke first when Jeff was in the hot seat but in the end, she always gave him comfort. She loved and cared deeply for her family and wanted the best for all of them. She kept the house in order and everybody in the right place. She was kind and smart, knew when to hold and when to fold. She was warm.

Jeff caught a quick glance at his father, a honest man. Much like his wife, his father loved and cared deeply for family. The Chief Financial Officer at Michigan Health Care Association was aging, but continued to work hard and expected Jeff, their only son, and his sisters to do the same. Jeff had always had a good relationship with his father. Jeff credited his father as being the one who taught him everything he needed to know, taught him how to be a man. They spent a lot of time together over the years. His father had truly been his mentor, his strength. The one who would correct him when he was wrong but give him a pat on the back when he'd done well. The one who kept him encouraged as his confidant and his friend.

His mother unfolded her arms, clasped her hands together and set them on the table. "What's happened to you? Are you trying to ruin your life?" she asked, her eyes cutting deeply into him. "The two of you could be in a Mexican jail."

Jeff realized he had been holding his breath, released the air caught in his throat and answered, "I know. I had no idea he was going to try to cheat the sales clerk."

"You are a journalist for goodness sake. That's what you do – ask question after question after question. Why don't you do the same with Robby? Are you afraid of what he might tell you?"

"He would not have told me that!"

"Well maybe he would have told you why he didn't have any luggage and why it was so important for him to get to the mall just a few hours after arriving. Was he planning to do this the entire trip? And who travels without luggage?"

"He had a bag–"

"This isn't really about bags or luggage, Jeff. I ask you again, are you trying to ruin your life?"

"No, Mom."

"You've got a great life and a great career as a sports writer for the *Detroit Daily* and your dad and I raised you to be an upstanding, honest citizen who conducts his business and affairs decently and orderly. We did not raise you to run around with common thieves."

Jeff Sr. put the cigar to his lips and exhaled. "We've warned you many times about keeping company with Robby."

"Well, we've been friends since we were children."

"And that means what?" his mother asked.

"It means we stick together no matter what."

"Does that mean you go to jail with him?"

Jeff didn't answer.

"Didn't think so."

"I got him out of it, didn't I?" he snapped.

Lynne shot Jeff a warning look, the first and last one she was going to give him.

"Sorry," he simply said.

"Where is he now? Did he take care of the fine? Have you even spoken to him to find out what happened?" she asked, folding her arms again.

"There was nothing else I could do for him."

"That's exactly our point! There is nothing else you can do for Robby."

"You better thank God you are not caught up in Robby's mess and I'd advise that you consider your ways. Find something to do and people headed in the same direction as you, to do it with," his father said.

"I owe him," Jeff said almost inaudible.

"You owe him?" Jeff Ryan Sr. said calmly. "Because he pulled you out the mud? Don't be ridiculous, son. In high school, we know you were saving part of your weekly allowance and giving it to Robby. In college, we know you were giving him clothes you were outgrowing. And what about driving with him around to fill out job applications and writing him letters of recommendation?

"What about you getting him a job at the *Detroit Daily*, stuffing papers and how about your parents digging deep into their pockets to ensure his grandfather had a proper burial. Since you're keeping score, don't you think it's about time to call it even?"

Jeff thought about some of the things he and Robby had been through over the years, good, bad and indifferent. It seemed that no matter what was going on with Robby, Robby was more concerned about Jeff's well being. It seemed like Robby was always saving Jeff from the worse and that meant Jeff owed him his loyalty. His parents didn't even know about the time he almost drowned. His father had paid for the boys to spend a couple of weeks at the CYO Boy's camp in Port Huron. He and some other boys went to the lake but Robby had stayed behind in the cabin because he had poison ivy. Jeff led the other boys to believe that he could swim and when they had begun rough housing; they pushed Jeff into the lake. And although he didn't come up immediately, the boys had thought Jeff was playing. When Jeff woke up, he was in Robby's arms, coughing up water and trying to breathe easy. Robby had later told him that he had sensed something bad was going to happen and decided to go out to the lake although he was ill.

"We know about the incident at summer camp." His father told him as if he was reading his mind. "When we came up to visit at the end of the first week, the counselors told us privately that Robby pulled you from the lake and performed CPR."

"You knew about that!" he said surprisingly and more so to himself.

His father simply nodded. "We enrolled you in swim classes that fall."

"Robby's had a rough, unfair life."

"Robby's not my son Jeff, you are," he pointed to him. "Stop trying to save him, he's not your responsibility. I'm concerned about him too but Robby has to make his own way; he's an adult."

"I'm hoping my life will help him change his."

His father rose from his chair, went over to Jeff and placed his hand on his shoulder. "It hasn't so far. Maybe *this* situation will change him instead." He left the room, taking his cigar and crystal cigar ashtray with him.

"Your dad's right," his mother continued. "We're not telling you to stop being Robby's friend, we not saying don't love him, care for him or even stop praying for him but you don't have to spend so much time with him, running around with him like you've been doing.

"You've been putting a lot of time and effort into trying to get him right… now that's unfair. You just be you and do what you are suppose to be doing."

Jeff nodded.

"I don't want to have this conversation with you again. Okay?" she didn't wait for an answer. "You've worked hard to get where you are and you're going even further. And you are too old to be in this predicament." She stood up. "Now come give your mom a hug." He did, holding onto her comfort. "I love you."

"I love you, too," he said still holding onto her. "And I'm sorry I wasn't using my head."

"Well tomorrow is a new day and thank God you have a chance to begin again. You now have a chance to start making better decisions, experiencing some better things. Hey, go and meet some new people."

"And do those things you love to do," his father added as he re-entered the kitchen." Jeff released his mother and went to his dad. "No father wants to see his child behind bars."

Standing face to face, he told him, "I know." They embraced.

Changing the subject he told him, "A good friend of mine at the Chicago Health Care Association told me that the *Chicago Daily* is looking for a sports editor. Why don't you consider it? You've been wanting to move up in your career, that opportunity just may be in Chicago."

"It may be," he said quietly.

"And I have one more request son?"

Jeff sighed, "what would that be, Dad?"

"That woman–"

"It's over."

Jeff unlocked the door of his high rise in downtown Detroit. As he entered, he inhaled the smell of old cigar smoke and frowned. Opening the living room windows, he lit a few scented candles and tried to relax. He took in the view overlooking the Detroit

River and a satisfying smile curved his lips but it soon faded when he remembered he had come home before it was time.

He pulled his saxophone from the sax stand and went to the door leading to his balcony. Unlatching and sliding the glass door open, he sat down and breathed in the river's air. Watching the water glisten under the moon, he began to play Dave Koz's, *It Might be You* but the sound just didn't flow through the instrument the way it should have; he couldn't concentrate, thinking about all the things that transpired in a matter of days.

He went inside, returned the saxophone to the sax stand and retrieved a Partagas Tubo cigar from the box sitting on the living room table. He also secured the cigar cutter and lighter in his hand and went out on the balcony again. Enjoying his cigar, Jeff thought about how he had worked hard to achieve success. His parents were right. While Jeff didn't want to lose everything, he wanted to see Robby do just as well and knew their relationship would never be the same. Jeff also knew he had been giving up his own life to make things happen and he could no longer do that.

At Fenton University, Jeff, who was a sports fan, had become the sports writer for the *Fenton Front Page News* and by his senior year, he worked as the sports editor. After graduation, he continued to work as the editor while interning at the *Detroit Daily*. Eventually his experience, aggression, professionalism and tenacity landed him a permanent position at the paper and Jeff had been there ever since.

Once again in his apartment, he decided to check his voice mail; perhaps some good news would come through the wire. It hadn't. Veronica left messages – the first two were about why she broke up with him but the last seven were begging him to take her back. He remembered the advice his father had given him about women. Like being patient and taking his time. And that he would meet a lot of women before choosing his bride so in the meantime he should focus on making the acquaintance and enjoy the ride while relationships evolved. It was all a process.

Jeff placed a block on Veronica's telephone number while self-consciously blocking out all women. He was giving up on love; it would no longer matter in his world. No more disappointments, no more hurt, no more heartache. No more money wasted on broken promises and no more time wasted on a "what if." This way, he could protect his own feelings.

He sucked in a breath and went into his office. Sitting behind his desk and logging onto his computer, he typed in the web address for the *Chicago Daily*, clicked on job opportunities, then sports editor and read the requirements. He had come to the time where he wanted to take his life back. Perhaps a change like this would be good. He attached his resume and just as he pressed the send button, the concierge called to say that his sisters, Bacari and Autumn, were on their way up.

Jeff's sister Bacari was the oldest child of the Ryan clan. She was four years Jeff's and his twin Autumn's senior. However, they grew up more like triplets as the resemblances were striking – from height, to complexion, to hair, to those silver, sleepy eyes. Since the siblings were children, they shared a bond so tight, it would have taken the Jaws of Life to pull them apart. Sure, Jeff was forced to play in the "princess castle" more times than he cared to remember but fortunately his sisters were tomboys and were okay with hopping fences, climbing trees, playing football – touch of course – and any game that resulted in getting grass stains and scratches. Just as long as their hair didn't get tangled, wet or simply, messed up, they were okay.

The siblings always attended the same schools and supported each other's activities. While Jeff excelled in baseball, his sisters were cheerleaders. He chose a career in journalism, they chose a career in business and cosmetology, eventually becoming owners of Classic Hair Designs. They stayed in constant communication. To make sure everyone did, once a week they'd get together for sibling night. That entailed meeting at Jeff's apartment or at his sister's condominium and spending the evening cooking, playing games, watching a movie or just talking.

Tonight wasn't an official sibling night. After Autumn got wind of Jeff's encounter with their parents, the girls wanted to get his side of the story. The threesome sat out on the balcony. Over Chinese food, he told them about what happened in Mexico. They, of course supported the way he handled the situation but they couldn't help but have some sympathy for Robby. The girls really loved Robby; not only because he use to beat up the bullies for them, but he had been a great friend to their brother despite growing up under unfortunate circumstances. They did believe that Robby cheated the sales clerk but they knew that through no fault of his own, he lacked guidance at the most important time in his life – his childhood years. Not that his behavior should be considered acceptable, but they'd wished Robby would have caught a different kind of break.

The siblings also talked about Veronica. In this case, no sympathy, just thankfulness that prayers were answered since Veronica was no longer in the picture. Bacari and Autumn felt that their brother could do much better and although he's had his share of ups and downs with women, they knew Jeff would find that special someone he was so deserving of. They'd even set Jeff up a few times but those relationships didn't work out but instead of giving up and giving in, they had yet another avenue for Jeff to socialize and meet new people, hopefully, a nice young lady.

Jeff cracked open his fortune cookie and repeated, "The Ballroom."

"Yes, The Ballroom," Bacari answered. "Remember a few years ago, Autumn and I took lessons?"

"Vaguely," he answered, reading his fortune.

Autumn took the slip of paper from him and asked, "Where were you under a rock!"

"I know about The Ballroom," he said defensively. "But I can't honestly say I remember a lot about you guys taking the lessons."

"It was way before The Ballroom was as popular but now, everybody's hip to it. In fact, we were there this past Friday and it was packed with people," Bacari said.

Jeff thought for a moment. "It must have been during the time…my early days after interning at…" Within moments, he had become lost in his own memories.

Jeff had stepped outside of the Detroit Daily relieved to be going home after having worked a few hours over time. He removed his suit coat and loosened his tie as he continued across the grounds and into the parking garage. Using his key chain to disarm the alarm and unlock the doors, he placed his briefcase on the back seat and hung his jacket on the hook.

"What's got you here so late?" someone asked.

He shut the door and looked up. There was a lady walking pass his car, pulling a travel cart. She stopped at the car next to his and opened the trunk. "Can I give you a hand with those boxes?" he asked walking toward her.

"No thanks, I can manage. These boxes aren't heavy," she said.

He helped her anyway, putting the boxes in her trunk. "Just tying up some loose ends before the work week ends," he responded to her question.

"Thanks for your help," she said closing her trunk. "Lamarr," she extended her hand.

He placed his hand in hers and firmly squeezed, "Jeff." Drawn in by her smile, Jeff thought about telling her but instead, he asked, "Are you new to the Daily? I've never seen you around here."

"No. I'm a sales consultant for the software company the Daily contracts with. Those boxes you put in my trunk contain software the Daily decided against. The others they agreed to use on a trial basis."

"But you did make a sale?"

"Not sure yet but at least my demonstration was enough to get them to pilot the product."

"I bet that smile could sell anything."

"Thank you," she responded coyly.

"Did...did I...say that...that out loud?" he stammered.

Lamarr blushed as she said softly, "You did." There was a comfortable silence. She spoke again. "I'm starving. Are there any cool places around here to–"

"Eat? Yes," he cut her off unintentionally, so he thought. "Off The River. It's not too far from here."

"Off The River?"

"It's a sports bar. Nachos, potato skins, buffalo wings, blooming onions, hamburgers, fries."

"Sounds good to me. If you don't have any plans, why don't you come along? I can use some company."

Jeff was lost for a moment. Who was this interesting woman and where did she come from?

Lamarr broke the silence. "I'm not asking for your hand in marriage Jeff, just two people getting together after work over a meal."

Something told him to make the acquaintance. "Okay Ms. Lamarr, we will go to Off The River for dinner."

"I'll follow you there."

Heart way deep into the relationship and at the point of no return, he hoped that maybe this could be it, the one, the only. They stayed connected for a while falling in love more and more with each passing day. One evening while he was visiting her at her home, her long lost 'friend' stopped by uninvited – or so Jeff assumed – begging for a second chance. She had simply stood in the entryway, staring at Jeff blankly.

"You were just in another place at that time." Autumn said knowing he had taken a trip down memory lane.

Jeff shook his head. "There was a time when I thought Lamarr and I would be forever."

Autumn read his fortune, "It says, expect something new on the horizon."

"How coincidental," Bacari added. "We have just the thing that'll prove that fortune right."

"Those things aren't really true," he commented as if they should know.

Autumn passed him a dark blue, professionally designed flier, the size of a standard invitation. "Play along little brother, it's–"

"Little brother?"

"Yeah, I came out first."

Jeff waved his hand at her as a blow off.

"It's the end of summer and this year's ballroom lessons and competition are getting underway. You should go."

Jeff scanned the information, detailing Detroit Club Style Ballroom lessons.

Bacari went on, encouraging him. "It would be a great way for you to meet new people, experience something new and learn how to dance. And the dance is exciting and fun."

Jeff shrugged.

"And we don't want to hear about you swearing off women, now that is being a lollipop," Autumn concluded.

"I'm not going to be too many more lollipops this month," Jeff said seriously. The room grew quiet for a moment before they all laughed.

"Robby is something else, calling you a lollipop." Bacari said shaking her head. "That's not right."

"Well you did tell him to grow up and you know Robby has to have the last word."

"Whatever, man, call me what you will. If I was so weak, where did I get the guts to stop them from taking him to jail? I wish you could have seen his face. I've never seen the look of fear on his face until that day." He stopped and then finished. "But I'm the lollipop."

"He was just defending himself," Bacari said trying to help Robby out. "You know he didn't mean it."

"He meant it. Robby always thought I was a wuss, he just never openly said it but I know he really does think I'm a softy. I bet Robby would switch places with me in a second."

"I bet," Autumn said getting up and walking toward Jeff. Standing behind him, she wrapped her arms around her twin. "Didn't mean any harm, I was just teasing."

"Get off of me," he told her jokingly.

Letting him go and nudging his shoulder, she told him, "Think about it brother."

"You know I've never been much of a dancer."

"We know but we've seen you move and at least you have rhythm.

"Yeah, I do," he said proudly.

"So what do you think?" Bacari asked.

"Ballroom lessons!" he pondered.

Autumn said, "They say, chances are, you'll fall in love at The Ballroom.

~

Chapter Three

Jade Stone studied the photograph of herself, her lips formed a satisfying curve. The photographer from *Fenton Front Page News* captured the very essence of her. It was the perfect picture to appear in the features section. The features reporter had come a few days before to interview her for an article about Jade's work as an instructor at the university's health and fitness center.

Jade couldn't take her eyes off of her own photos as she viewed each one carefully. Her jet-black hair, resting at her jaw line, was styled so that it covered the left side of her face and with the right amount of light, the camera brought out the green in her eyes. Her mouth, a slight pout, her cheeks dimpled. Amber, her younger sister, had made the right choice selecting an outfit for the full shot photos. A pair of designer, low rise workout capris, a cardio combat, short sport top and a pair of the most popular fitness shoes – all by Nike – perfect for showing off her muscular, athletic build on her mere five-foot three inch frame.

Using her fingertips to move hair off of her face and letting it fall back into place – she did this often, Jade gave the photos back to the photographer. "Thank you. You take excellent photos," she told him.

Blood rushed to his face and it took a moment for him to respond but finally, he managed to say, "You're welcome. Thanks."

Jade was satisfied with the effect she had over him and almost all the men she had come in contact with. She walked toward the thermostat and pretended to be adjusting the air. Jade heard the photographer inhale and she could almost feel his eyes burning into her back. Smirking, she asked, "When can I expect to see the article in the Front Page?"

"The next issue, next month."

She faced him and nodded. "Great! I look forward to reading it. I am ever so grateful for the opportunity to be featured. I hope that it will encourage more faculty and students to sign up for my classes."

The photographer searched for something to say before he spoke again. "You have a nice – you have a very nice–"

"A nice what?" she urged.

"A nice workout room," he said quickly.

Still satisfied, she offered, "I can show you around the place if you like. This state-of-the-art fitness center is one of the best features on Fenton University's campus."

"I'd love to see the place – sometime – but I have to take more photos for another assignment. I just stopped by to get the thumbs up on your photos before they go to print." He was reminding himself, not her.

Flipping her hair and letting it fall back into place, she shrugged. "Okay, come back and see me sometime. I'd be more than happy to show you around."

"Sounds good. You know Mrs. Stone–"

"Ms. Stone. Jade, please."

"Jade. You're very gorgeous and I think you should be a model."

"You really think so?"

"I do."

"You know, once upon a time, as a teenager, I dated a guy who told me the same thing! And with his pushing, I got into it. I did get enough assignments to build a portfolio but after we broke up, I lost interest and moved on to something else." She glanced at her watch.

"Am I keeping you from something?"

"Not at all. My first class of the semester starts in about an hour, just making sure I stay on schedule."

He extended his hand, she accepted. "Good seeing you again."

"Likewise," she responded, walking him to the door.

Once he was gone, she looked around the room and recalled the journey that got her here. Jade's high school sweetheart in senior year had convinced her to go to Fenton University because that's where he was going. Not exactly sure what to study, she changed majors under each sweetheart's admonishment – from acting, to law, to engineering, to music to finance. Finally, after six years, she earned a Bachelor of Science in Exercise Science. Since, yet another sweetheart convinced her that health and fitness was a way of life and that's what he was studying. Even after the split, there was another sweetheart there to make sure she earned her American Council of Exercise Certificate and certification as a group fitness instructor. Eventually, she just fell in love with her work.

Contracting with Motor City Fitness Club allowed her to work at Motown Fitness, several automotive plants, the Michigan Health Care Association, a senior citizens residence and a few neighborhood community centers before she heard of Fenton University's plans to build a state-of-the art-fitness center. Using her networking skills, by the time the doors opened, she was among those chosen for the job, along with her sister who would work as her assistant.

Jade and Amber had spent some time setting up the room. Storage bins had been neatly pushed against the walls. Each one contained exercise equipment students would need: bands, hand weights, jump ropes, plush mats. There was even a lost and found bin. Next to the storage bins were stair steps neatly stacked and next to the stair steps, the medicine ball rack. On the other side of the room were the electronic scales and what was a seating area of the sorts, a couple of burgundy leather chairs in-between a small glass coffee table containing issues of a few health and fitness magazines. There was also a water cooler. And an added touch, beyond their control, was the floor-to ceiling windows and a breathtaking view of the campus.

Helping herself to a cup of water, she sat on one of the chairs just as Amber came into the room, rolling a Coach navy blue multi-wheeled traveler behind her.

"Hi, sister," Amber greeted her.

"Hi, sister," Jade responded. "Have everything we need for today?"

"Everything!" she answered. "How did it go with the photographer?"

"Well, the photos looked great. I can't wait to see them and the article in print."

Amber grinned. "Did you mention your partner?"

Jade stood up and tossed her empty cup in a wastebasket. Walking toward her sister, she stepped in front of her and embraced her. "Now you know I mentioned you. How could I not?"

Amber broke out of her embrace. "You better had mentioned me," she said, pushing her playfully.

Jade smoothed the loose ends of Amber's hair in place. "I think you'll be pleased with the article but moreover, I'm praying that it'll make more people health conscious and of course bring us more students."

"Oh, I'm sure it will. You keep working them out, they keep seeing results, they'll keep coming back and bringing others."

"I know we just need some time. It's only been about three years." Glancing at her watch she said, "Well this is it! About fifteen people will be filing in shortly. Are you ready for the first of six sessions today?"

"About as ready as I'm going to be."

"Did you grab the tape measures off of my desk?"

Unzipping the travel bag, she quickly searched the contents. "You actually left them on my desk but I got them."

Jade let out a breath. "All right then, here we go!"

As the students started filing in, Amber greeted them at the door, welcoming them and verifying their registration against the list the university had faxed to their office. Jade stood further inside of the room, welcoming them as well. She also watched their body language closely to get a feel of each one's comfort level and a way to "determine" their personality. She also made note of body types, including all shapes and sizes. Flipping her hair, she couldn't help but check out their expression toward her. Some were double takes, some curiosity, some eye rolls, a few blushes and a couple of neutrals.

Jade and Amber had waited for a few stragglers to arrive before Jade introduced herself, shared her credentials and expertise and then introduced Amber who had shared her information. Students had then introduced themselves. Upon Jade's request, each one shared an interesting fact about themselves. She had warned them that while most times both she and Amber would lead sessions, there may be times when they'd see one and not the other.

Jade continued the session with an overview that included the fitness center's history and important places in the center, such as the locker rooms and showers, her office and the café which sold nutritional foods and snacks only, main lobby and breakout areas. She explained what the students could expect and what staff expected from students, which included guidelines, policies and procedures.

Jade reiterated class days and times and gave her office hours. She also talked about the benefits of taking her class and other miscellaneous information, like, the equipment and usage of the room and usage of the center. She had told them about their option of getting a locker Amber would assign to them along with a combination lock. Most of what was discussed, along with important forms was distributed to them in a Fenton University Fitness Center folder.

After answering a few questions, Jade and Amber then took some time privately taking the student's measurements – chest, stomach, thighs and weight – while they discussed their purpose for signing up and results they wanted to accomplish. Once the last measurement was taken, Amber gave each student a small but fancy journal to log the foods they ate. Jade admonished them to also record the time they ate and how they felt physically after eating. Jade told them that she would meet with them every other week to review their journal with them and advise according to their expectations. With just fifteen minutes left, Jade and Amber led the class in a low impact aerobic session before commending them on a job well done. She had admonished them to give themselves a round of applause because while some were cozy in their homes on their sofa, they were here choosing a healthier lifestyle.

Five more sessions later, the end of the day had finally come to a close and an exhausted Jade and Amber began straightening up the room while critiquing each session. They talked about what worked, what didn't and what they could do differently next time. They talked about the students – the comedians, the serious, the way too serious, the doubters, those in between, which ones were in it for the long haul, which ones would probably drop out.

Amber let out a breath and said to Jade, "I've been waiting all day to give you something."

"What?" Jade asked while examining a wristband and tossing it into the lost and found bin.

Amber walked over to her traveler and pulled out the dark blue, professionally designed flier, the size of a standard invitation to The Ballroom. Jade was already heading her way when they met in the middle of the room. "Here," Amber said smiling and giving Jade the flier.

Flipping her hair, Jade grabbed the flier and read it.

Amber continued, "I know how much you love being a social butterfly and when I read this, I instantly thought of you. It seems like it'll be a lot of fun."

"I've heard of The Ballroom but I didn't know about the lessons – excuse me, Detroit Club Style Ballroom. This place is located downtown, right?"

"In the heart of it."

"This does sound like fun and a lot of men to choose from." Jade noticed her sister's frown. "Well, anyway," she said. "Our girlfriends know about everything happening in and around the city, why hadn't they mentioned this?"

"*Your* friends not *mine*."

"How did you find out about it?"

"*My* friends and I were there last weekend and I picked up the flier."

Jade took a few steps back and re-read the flier. "I want to go." She said hesitantly.

"But?"

"But why didn't my so-called friends tell me about it?"

"You'll have to ask them."

"I haven't been out with them lately. I call, they don't return my calls. I send e-mails, they go unanswered. And when I finally reach somebody, they claim to be so busy but later I hear about what a great and wonderful time they had without me. I know it, they're avoiding me. Why?"

Amber studied her sister for a moment and then answered, "I think you know the answer to that Jade."

Jade threw her hands up. "Why am I always punished because I'm so beautiful, I mean, I can't help it that I have the looks and a fabulous body to go with it. It's not my fault that I get all the attention and they don't. They always get mad at me when guys fuss all over me and then they stop talking to me. They should get over it. Standing here in all my glory and all they can do is envy all of this." She managed to catch her breath before she finished. "I can't help it how others respond. They should get over it."

"Did you just hear yourself?"

Jade didn't answer.

"Did you just hear yourself?"

Jade looked out the window, the sun had set, ushering in dusk. She faced her sister. "We don't spend enough time together outside of work, we should do this together, you know, as sisters, me and you."

Amber shook her head, "No thanks!"

"Not you, too."

Amber simply stared at her sister.

"You look just like me," she said matter-of-factly.

Amber said nothing.

Looking at the flier, taking a few more steps back, Jade said, "Once upon a time as a young adult–"

"You dated a guy who told you to dance and you did but then the relationship soured and you stopped dancing."

Flipping her hair, she winked at her sister.

"That's all you got, huh?"

"That's all I need."

"That's unhealthy."

"You know why I'm like this," Jade yelled.

"I know it's an over-the-top, weak excuse."

"Easy for you to say Amber always been cute as a button, Stone."

Amber walked to her sister, grabbed her shoulders and shook her, the flier falling at Jade's feet. "Everything doesn't have to be about a man, does it?"

"I need a crutch!"

"You need an excuse."

Jade pushed Amber's hands off of her shoulders.

Amber grabbed her again and this time pushed her slowly around in a circle, giving her a full view of each corner of the room as she spoke, "You did all of this Jade Stone, not some man, not your looks, not your body but your brain. Yes, some know-it-all man got the ball rolling but you passed the classes, you took the test, you made contacts, you, you, you!"

"Is everything all right in here?" The women turned at the sound of one of the security guard's voices. It was Sparky, a man they had known since they started working at the center.

"Everything's fine," Amber answered. Realizing that she was still holding on to Jade, she let her go.

"Yeah, everything's fine," Jade said, assuring the guard.

"I can walk you ladies to your car," he told them as he did all the time.

"Of course," Jade said. "In a few minutes."

Amber walked over to her traveler, organized the contents and zipped it.

"I'll meet you ladies at the employee entrance," he said giving both a once-over before walking away.

Amber began to pull her bag and stopped at the door. "They say chances are you'll fall in love at The Ballroom. I hope you fall in love with yourself. I'll meet you at the entrance."

Jade fought back tears and picked up the flier. Trilling it in her fingers, Jade thought about the encounter she just had with Amber. She knew that while it was true that she got more attention than her friends, in her own way, Jade made sure that that happened. Her friends would never understand why she had to be noticed. And, regarding Amber, she just didn't understand that every woman needed a man for some reason or another. Yes, she did accomplish a lot on her own but she couldn't have done it without them, right? Oh, and needing them wasn't an excuse, was it?

Turning off the light, she closed the door and walked to her office. Logging off her computer and grabbing her personal belongings, she met up with Amber at the entrance. The sisters embraced and kissed each other on the cheek. There are just some things that Amber would never understand, Jade thought, but she loved her anyway. Still, Jade pulled Amber's hand inside of hers as Sparky escorted them through the parking structure and to their cars. Jade climbed into her car, Amber into hers and Sparky headed back toward the building. Amber waved and drove off.

Jade glanced at the flier one last time. Once upon a time, just this summer, a guy she was dating told her to take up rollerblading with him. She did, but summer was coming to a close and well, so was their relationship. Amber had said that chances are you'll fall in love at The Ballroom, well, here was her chance.

~

Chapter Four

Ivan James knew it was eight o'clock because every morning at this time, James Brown's *It's a Man's World* came blaring through the speakers he had installed in each room for no other reason but to remind him of his exact place in the world.

Pushing back his white, plush silk blanket and then the matching silk sheets on his king-sized waterbed, he sat up on the edge and slid his feet into his brown Polo Ralph Lauren Jaguar slippers. They matched his Polo Ralph Lauren pajamas and robe perfectly.

Taking a quick glance out of his bedroom window, he marveled at the sunrise. Although a little foggy, he knew it was going to be a great day. The view from his high-rise apartment allowed him to see Windsor, Canada, the Detroit River and the Detroit skyline was one of the reasons. How bad could life be from where he stood?

The song played continuously as he plunged into his day, just like most days. Going into the bathroom, his reflection stopped him and he winced then caught himself because he knew that after he finished putting his package together, it would make up for what he lacked in looks, affording him charm, appeal. He ran his hand over his clean-shaven head and then started and ended his ritual of showering and shaving in an hour.

In his dressing room, Ivan sung the chorus as he dressed his five-foot four frame in a cranberry Salvatore Ferragamo pique polo, a pair of Khaki Ferragamo pants and matching reversible belt. Slipping his feet into a pair of black sache loafers also by Ferragamo, it was time for him to accessorize. Ivan's watch, pendant, bracelet, diamond ring, and an earring were all by Tiffany & Company.

Ivan stepped in front of his full-length mirrors and posed a few times before he gave himself approval. Then he sprayed on his favorite fragrance, of course by Ferragamo. The doorbell rang, the music stopped. Breakfast was at his door.

Nine-thirty.

Credit Card Lady brought him breakfast from Adorable Dough Café, same time, everyday. He let her in and made small talk as she giggled the entire time. Then, over breakfast, he forced himself to dazzle her enough to keep her near. Breakfast wasn't important but her paying the credit card bill was. An hour later, he gave her next month's bill, thanked her for breakfast and made sure she'd return tomorrow.

Ten-thirty.

Closing the door behind her, he went into the living room and turned on his 47" flat-panel LCD high-definition television set, flipping to the weather channel, just to see if he would be able to drive with the top down. He turned the set off and went into his study, collecting all of his bills – car note, insurance, cellular, BlackBerry and a few others. He had about an hour to deliver them to each woman responsible for paying them. Getting his keys, he was out the door and headed toward the garage. That's when Lunch Lady called to confirm their noon lunch date. He made sure he had her bill in hand.

In the garage, he disarmed his Le Mans Blue Metallic Corvette. Climbing in, he started the car, lowered the top and drove out of the garage.

By one-thirty, Ivan was finished with lunch, back in his Corvette and driving to visit his brother. He could see the brick building just ahead of him and the name that read, I. James Service Center. As he pulled into a parking space, he watched customers coming and going. He thought about how business must be good. He also couldn't help but wonder had he made a mistake, had he been acting simple. A while ago, he partnered with his brother who had fired him and he still couldn't understand why his brother had done that to flesh and blood. It didn't hurt their personal relationship though as they kept in touch over the telephone, but it had been a while since he'd visited his brother and his family. Neither had he been to the service center in a while, the place his brother promised would be theirs. Nonetheless, today, he just wanted to see his brother, he didn't know why.

He breezed through the station as if the staff and customers should be impressed with him. The owner's brother did not move the manager, the mechanics and maintenance but he gave them a courteous greeting anyway. The receptionist and a few of the women customers, however, either looked twice or found themselves holding their breath. Ivan was more than satisfied at the response and made a mental note to flirt with the receptionist on the way out.

Reaching the back of the station, he stopped at his brother's office door, which was slightly ajar. Raising a fist to knock, he took a deep breath and let it out.

"Come in Ivan," he heard his brother say.

Pushing it open and closing it behind him, he asked, "How did you–"

"I know everything that goes on under this roof. Now, how can I help you?" he asked, raising from his desk and heading toward his brother.

Ivan watched him approach and wondered why God had given his brother, five years older than him, looks and height with a head full of hair. Ivan had started to lose his at an early age. He wanted to ask but instead he said, "What's up Ian! I just thought I'd come check you out."

Ian reached out and gave Ivan a man's hug but felt Ivan's body tense. For a second, he blamed himself for how Ivan had turned out but then he remembered how hard he'd tried for both of them, Ivan even more.

"Please sit," he told him, motioning to the chair in front of his desk as he leaned on the edge of it. "I was in the middle of finishing up payroll."

"Business must be good."

"And getting better every day. I'm thankful for how things turned out."

"The Mrs. and those little ones," Ivan stated.

"They're wonderful," he said as the telephone rang. "Excuse me." Ian reached for the telephone and spent several minutes handling business before continuing his conversation about his family. He had brought Ivan up to date. "You should stop by, Ivan, they'd really like to see you." Ivan said nothing at first and then nodded. Not quite sure how to read it, Ian continued. "You're looking prosperous. What have you been up to?"

Ivan shifted his weight. Ivan knew Ian's angle and Ian was the only man on earth who could make him squirm. "Well, you know. I umm. I'm Ivan James, I can't be nothing but all right."

"I asked what's going on with you?"

"Well, you know. I umm. I'm Ivan James, same old same, just a different day, you know!"

The telephone rang again. Ian handled the call and noted Ivan's irritation. When he finished his call, he asked, "What brings you here?"

"As I said earlier, I was just coming to check you out!"

"In the middle of the afternoon? You must have the day off or are you on lunch?"

Ivan shifted his weight again. Ian was the only man on earth who could see right through him. Ivan thought he'd make a smooth exit while he had the opportunity, especially since the telephone rang yet again. "I can see you're busy, I should just let you go."

Ian decided to trump him, "Okay." He answered the call and noted that Ivan hadn't moved from his seat. He finished the call.

"Business must really be good."

Ian simply nodded.

"I can tell. Give me a job!"

"Are you asking me for a job?"

"You know, I'm Ivan James, I don't ask questions but I do get results," he said jokingly but really wasn't.

"Fix your life."

"Cut me some slack, Bro!"

"Why, Ivan? Tired of using women or did they finally wake up?"

"I'm not using them," he said defensively. "I can't help it if they want to take care of me."

"You're thirty-five years old Ivan. When are you going to take care of you, you know, be a man?"

Ivan felt his anger rising and forced himself to control it. "I didn't come here to argue Ian, I came here to–"

"Disrupt my business because you're blood and you're entitled? I started the business with you in management. You came when you wanted, you left when you wanted, you were always holed up in the office with some woman. I was trying to run a business and give you a job in the process–"

"You weren't supposed to let me go. I thought you'd hang in there for me."

Ian responded sarcastically, "You're right, I was supposed to pay you for work you weren't doing. Now that *does* make a lot of sense."

"You know what I mean, Ian."

This time when the telephone rang, Ian ignored the call. "You want easy. You want everything given to you and life doesn't work that way. You have to earn a living. You have to work hard to get things you want."

"I am your brother," he said, enunciating each word.

"And I'm your brother, too. Cut me some slack; hang in there for me. The sooner you learn that the sun doesn't rise, shine, and set on you, the better off you'll be."

Ivan flashed the diamond ring sparkling on his pinky finger. "It's shining to me."

"Material things some woman brought you is your measurement of success? It's going to catch up with you real soon."

"Doubt it. I'm Ivan James."

"How do you get to sleep at night?"

"Comfortably under my one hundred and fifty seven dollar silk sheets, a different color for each week of the month."

Ian shook his head. "I may not live for free in another woman's high rise but I purchased a nice house with my own money for my loving wife and children. I may not dress like a million bucks but my business brings in that kind of revenue, plus, each year.

"And I don't have a problem meeting clients in my three hundred dollar suits or coming to the office in my Dockers that I purchased with my hard earned money. I may not have a fancy sports car that some other woman is paying for but I take joy in driving my SUV, a SUV I bought with my own money."

Ivan stared at Ian like he was considering Ian's truth.

"Look, I'm here to help, it's the last time I'm saying it."

"You don't come into my house making demands, man. You better come correct. Now, there are no openings at this time. When one becomes available, I'll let you know and you can apply–"

"Apply!"

"Yeah, like send in a resume online. And if you qualify, my manager will call you and set up an interview."

"You make me sick, Ian."

As Ivan stood to leave, Ian grabbed Ivan by the neck and squeezed just enough to hear him gasp. "Now you wait a minute. This isn't going to be another one of your outbursts and you are not leaving here with your butt on your shoulders." Releasing just a little pressure, Ian continued, "don't you ever forget who did the best he could raising you! I was a teenager myself, trying to find my way in the world and keep an eye on you, too. Everything I did was for you Ivan – in spite of."

He released Ivan's neck but continued, "and somehow I was able to pull myself up by my bootstraps and make an honest living. Working as a car mechanic in this man's back yard and in that man's garage to working in another man's station until I was finally able to open my own station. I didn't allow the past to keep me from a successful future. Even found a wonderful woman to marry me and give me girls. You chose not to stay the course, not me.

"I. James Service Center does not have any job openings at this time. I encourage you to visit our Web site for future openings. If there is an opening, you may send your resume online and if you qualify, my manager will contact you for an interview."

Ivan absently smoothed out his shirt and headed toward the door.

"Ivan," Ian called.

Ivan stopped but didn't face his brother.

"Look at me, Ivan," he demanded.

Ivan slowly turned.

Ian could see that Ivan's eyes had turned red but he knew his brother would not release his anger. "Next year I plan to open another shop and I could use a manager. One of my mechanics wants it bad and he just may get it if my brother doesn't get his self together."

Ivan straightened his shoulders and nodded.

"I've done all I could and I owe you nothing but to love you and I do but if you ever spit venom in my face again, I won't loosen my grip next time."

Ivan said okay but it was barely audible. He wanted so badly to hold Ian and cry his heart out and beg Ian to make the pain go away just as he did when they were growing up. However, he was Ivan James, right? He couldn't just break down, not even for Ian, the one who would understand the most but still he had to be strong. "That's what Ian always told me, to be strong."

"But I never said be a fool, and I never said use people to your advantage and I never said bottle things up."

"You must have heard me. I was thinking to myself."

"I wish you would go see—"

"I'm fine Ian, really I am." Looking at his watch, then he said, "I gotta run, Bro. I have a couple of appointments." With that, Ian picked up his ringing telephone and Ivan was gone from Ian's office. He slipped into the men's room to regain his composure, go back into the world and be that suave man everyone expected to see.

Breezing back through the service center as if his encounter with Ian had been like a walk in the park, he stopped by the receptionist's desk to flatter her long enough for the manager to appear and shoot her a look as customers patiently waited to cash out. She abruptly gave him her business card and shooed him away. Ivan was satisfied and back in the game. Climbing into his Corvette, he visited a few more of his friends before returning home.

Five o'clock.

He'd catch the evening news, wait for his evening company to arrive and try to block out what Ian had told him several hours earlier. Opening the door to his apartment, he grimaced. The last person he was in the mood for was the woman keeping this roof over his head. She was aware of his position but for some reason played along with him. Ivan presumed that she needed him as much as he needed her and admittedly for the wrong reasons.

Lease Lady escorted Ivan to the table set romantically for two. Dimming the lights and drawing the blinds in the dining room so that the illumination of the candlelight would be sufficient, she told him to freshen up, dinner would be ready soon. He wanted her out of his – her apartment but instead, he obliged. Besides, Ivan needed some time to strategize her exit before seven thirty and he had to get that key from her.

Sitting back at the table, Ivan behaved the way he knew she had wanted – attentive, loving, caring, thoughtful. He even marveled over the meal and devoured seconds. The clock was ticking and he offered to help her clean up quickly. He threw her off guard; he knew it. Now for the keys.

On the sofa, over the third glass of White Zinfandel, he was closer to getting the keys. "You surprised me with a dinner tonight but I wouldn't be able to return the favor."

"Why not?"

"Because," he said, kissing her nose. "Because, you have a key and that means you can come in anytime and you could spoil the surprise."

"I don't want to spoil the surprise," she said sipping her wine.

He held out his hand. "Come on, sweetheart."

"Do you think I'm going to come in here and harm you?"

"The keys, princess," he cooed, hand still out.

"I don't want you dead. I want you to be my only one."

"I am your only one."

"You are a liar." Finishing her wine, she set her glass down, picked up her purse and fished through it for the keys. Pulling them out, she placed them in his hand.

"I love you," he said without feeling while looking at the clock.

Seven-twenty.

"Just remember that I can get a set from property management. The leasing agreement is in my name." She headed for the door and he immediately fell in step behind her. She opened the door and stepped on the other side of it.

"Wait!" he said grabbing her, kissing her long and hard. She pulled back and smirked, staring him straight in the eyes. It chilled him because he couldn't read it, neither was it an expression he had ever seen from her but he didn't have time to try to figure it out.

Seven twenty-six.

She walked to the elevators and pressed the down button. He prayed that she wouldn't run into Evening Lady. Closing the door, he quickly called the manager of property management at her home. He had five, maybe six minutes to make her promise not to give the key to Lease Lady.

Seven-thirty.

The concierge called, Evening Lady had arrived. He told him to send her up.

Ivan let her in and realized that he had forgotten about the wine glasses and swiftly removed them. He wasn't sure if Evening Lady noticed them. If she did, she didn't flinch. He guessed she had something else on her mind because after a while, she gave him a dark blue, professionally designed flier, the size of a standard invitation. It was to The Ballroom and Evening Lady thought it would be a good idea if they took the lessons together. He was used to convincing ladies why they should, now he had to convince this lady why they shouldn't. He certainly was going – new opportunity, new adventure, new territory, new phase, another game.

His convincing worked. As far as she was concerned, because of his hectic schedule, they'd wait until next year to take the lessons. He made a mental note to call Miscellaneous Lady, just to say goodnight and to get the $150 dollars for the twenty-nine sessions. Evening Lady's work was done for the day and Ivan escorted her to his door and sighed. She had told him something about chances are you'll fall in love at The Ballroom. If only he knew what love was.

~

Chapter Five

The Ballroom was famous for it's all night dance experience – from Salsa to Tango to the Waltz. If you weren't dancing, you were watching in awe while mingling with who's who in the city.

Uniquely decorated with indigo furnishings and lights blended with every shade of blue there was – from azure and cobalt to royal and sapphire and Prussian to midnight and periwinkle.

The Ballroom had two levels. The first level, of course was complete with immense dance floors on either side of the D.J.'s booth, surrounded by plush seating, bar chairs and tables and a comfortable lounge in the back of the club. The second level belonged to Skye's, known to serve the best seafood in town. Skye's also had banquet rooms for private parties and provided catering. Dining in the restaurant was perhaps the main attraction as floor-to-ceiling windows allowed diners an awesome view of The Ballroom to watch the dancers.

Club-goers, along with the twenty students who signed up for the lessons, were moving about in the lounge, sitting near or standing on the dance floor, or practicing steps, waiting anxiously for the lessons to get underway. Brooke, who was usually calm and mentally ready to take on any challenge, was experiencing anxiety. Walking pass the cherry wood high-dining tables with indigo bar-height chairs, she headed toward an empty table next to the dance floor. Sitting in one of the available chairs facing the dance floor, she tried reminding herself not to take it too seriously and to have fun.

She noticed a very handsome man heading in her direction. The guy appeared to be just as anxious as she. He sat at the table next to hers, smelling of Issey Miyake cologne. He simply gave a courteous smile, turned his attention toward the dance floor and started bobbing his head to the non-strict ballroom music. *That's Detroit*, she thought, referring to how some men are unfriendly toward women they didn't know. However, she thought that maybe he was a little shy or maybe she's the only one who was just interested or maybe she just felt a need to make a friend. If she could only get a hello, the rest would fall into place.

Finally, he turned his attention to Brooke. She smiled and said, "Hi."

"Hello," he answered. "How are you?"

She pushed aside the indigo glass candleholder. "I'm fine thanks, and yourself?"

"I'm good."

"I'm Brooke," she offered.

Getting up from his chair and walking to her, he said, "Jeff."

She took his offered hand in hers and held it for a moment, intentionally longer than normal. "It's nice to meet you, Jeff."

"Likewise," he responded as he sat in a chair next to her but still facing the dance floor. "First time?"

"Yes, how about you?"

"First time. How did you find out about the lessons and what made you decide to come out?"

"I've heard about this place when they first opened but I have to admit taking the lessons was the furthest from my mind until my best friend convinced me to take them. You?"

"My sisters. They took the lessons a few years back and came here often but like you, taking the lessons was the furthest from my mind. They convinced me."

"Sounds like we both thought it wasn't such a bad idea."

"Nope, it's not a bad idea at all. Is your best friend taking the lessons with you?"

"No, she claims to have two left feet. I guess she does but anyway, I'm taking it alone, you?"

"I'm on my own too."

"Well, perhaps we could be partners!" She said quickly as if getting it off her chest.

Jeff heard her talking but he didn't hear what she said. The lone figure walking in their direction had distracted him.

Brooke followed Jeff's gaze and saw where it rested. She had to admit, that the woman was strikingly beautiful and with that body, she had to be in somebody's gym regularly. Brooke noted Jeff using non-verbal communication to get her to join them but if she wasn't mistaken, Glamour Girl was already on her way. When she approached, they all said "hello" at the same time.

Jeff stood. "I'm Jeff, this is Brooke and you are?"

She shook both of their hands. "I'm Jade."

"Pleasure meeting you Jade. Please sit down," he said pulling out and pushing her chair in once she was seated.

"Thank you," she said. "Have you guys ever been here before?"

"First time for both of us," Brooke answered.

"Yeah, we just met a few moments ago," Jeff added.

She flipped her hair. "That's cool. I came alone as well and I was hoping I'd see some friendly faces. I guess you guys are it. The friendliest I've seen so far."

"First time?" Brooke asked.

Jade flipped her hair and nodded. "My sister Amber, talked me into it. She'd thought it would be a great way to meet people, I guess. What about you guys?"

Drawn in by her dimpled cheeks, visible whether she smiled or not, he thought, *I bet those dimples could introduce you to anybody.* "Well, Brooke's friend talked her into it and my sisters talked me into it."

"Oh yeah? How many sisters do you have?"

"Just two."

"Any brothers?"

"No, one of my sisters is my twin and the other is older."

"Wow, you have a twin?" Jade confirmed.

Jeff nodded. "What about you Brooke? Any brothers or sisters?"

Brooke hesitated before answering. "No. I'm an only child."

"Amber's my only sibling and she's younger by about two years."

"I hope you're saving this seat for me!"

The threesome abruptly focused on the well-dressed man making the statement.

"Ivan James," he really said to Jade. "I saw you at the registration table but you got away from me before I could catch you."

"Caught!" she said grinning while flipping her hair. "Please have a seat. This is Brooke and Jeff."

He shook both of their hands. "Ivan James," he said, just in case they hadn't heard him the first time. Jeff and Brooke exchanged glances but said nothing. "And what's your name good-looking?"

"Jade," she blushed.

He brushed her hair away from her face and looked into her eyes, "How fitting."

"Is that a compliment?"

"It is."

"Well in that case, thanks."

"For sure."

The music stopped.

Everyone watched the woman saunter onto the dance floor. Hair pulled neatly in a bun, the woman sported an orange blouse, matching skirt and a pair of tan lady's teaching shoes with a squared Cuban heel. She flashed a bright smile; her teeth covered with neon braces and introduced herself as Louisa, their instructor. She then introduced her assistant, Emilio. The music started playing again and she and Emilio gave the students a taste of what to expect. When they finished the dance, it seemed as if each student let out a sigh of relief, a feeling that they could do it and couldn't wait to get started.

Louisa gathered the class around the dance floor. Once everyone was in place, she asked each one to introduce themselves and then gave them and the spectators the housekeeping rules. She also told the class about the much anticipated, much talked about spring competition, open for everyone around town to witness, including the participant's family and friends.

The competition guidelines were as follows: Assuming that all twenty students participate, they should arrive at The Ballroom no later than six-thirty in the evening to register. Three sets of competing partners would start at seven o'clock. In the first set, all ten couples would dance but only six couples would advance to the second set. Following the second set, three couples would be eliminated leaving the remaining three to compete in the third and final set. These competitors would be allowed to provide the D.J. with music they prepared, which should be three to five minutes long. The competition would be judged by first, second and third place finalists from the previous year.

Cash prizes would be awarded to the third place winners in the amount of one thousand dollars, for the second place winners in the amount of three thousand dollars and first place winners, five thousand dollars. And all winners would be invited to judge next year's competition. After the competition, The Ballroom will acknowledge all participants and then the floor belongs to them before it'll open up to all guests.

Louisa told the class that they had the choice of selecting a partner for the competition at a later date or she could match them up. Meanwhile, they would switch partners after each song in order to find which partner would work out best and also to be able to go anywhere to dance with anyone. Louisa had then spent some time answering questions before she said, "Now, grab a partner for now and just have fun learning the dance.

As the students moved about, Louisa and Emilio closely observed how the students went about selecting a partner.

Ivan quickly but smoothly grabbed Jade's arm and pulled her as close to him as he could. He whispered in her ear, "You're my partner tonight and you're my partner for the competition."

She giggled, "Okay by me."

"Would you like to be my partner?" Jeff asked Brooke after watching the exchange between Ivan and Jade.

"Sure," she said lightly.

Several minutes had passed when Emilio stepped forward and said, "We presume that each of you have a dance partner, right?"

"Yes," the class answered.

"Good! How were you asked or how did you ask?" he questioned them.

The short guy sporting a pair of Cartier shades said, "I asked her if she already had a partner and she said no so I asked her if she would like to partner up with me."

Emilio's expression indicated that that was almost all right.

The petite lady sporting a Mohawk answered next. "We sort of asked each other at the same time."

Emilio's expression indicated that that probably wasn't good.

"I first introduced myself to the young lady and then asked her if she would like to dance," The businessman answered with confidence.

Emilio waved his hand from side to side. "Brooke? How were you asked?"

"I actually asked my partner first but I don't think he heard me. However, he ended up asking me if I wanted to be his partner," Brooke answered. She noticed the surprised, yet baffled look on Jeff's face and wondered if she had said too much. Perhaps she should have left out the part about her asking him first.

Emilio raised an eyebrow. "Ivan? How did you ask Jade?"

Ivan poked his chest out slightly and said as if Emilio should know, "I just pulled her close to me and told her that she was going to be my partner."

Emilio's expression was unreadable. "Ladies, please form a straight line on the floor." All of the women quickly fell into place and Louisa lined up with them. Men, please, form a straight line on the opposite side but make sure that you are in front of your partner." The men fell quickly into place.

Emilio stood in front of Louisa. "Asking for a dance is very important because it's part of etiquette.

"First, the man always approaches the lady." He reached out his hand to Louisa but she didn't receive his hand. Addressing the class, he continued. "Second, the man politely asks the lady if she would like to dance." He turned his attention to Louisa. "Would you like to dance?"

Louisa extended her hand and placed it in Emilio's.

"By giving me her hand she has said yes. And now I can lead her to the dance floor," he concluded.

Deep sighs could be heard throughout the class as if most had been holding their breath.

"I do not want to see any grabbing, demanding, pushing or pulling. Ask the lady the exact way you've learned in this class. It is the proper way. Treat the lady like a lady and ladies, allow him to treat you like a lady."

"Is everyone clear?" Louisa asked.

"Yes," the class responded.

Businessman raised his hand and asked, "What will the lady do if the answer is no?"

"When you ask her properly, the answer will never be no," Emilio stated.

"Never?"

"I can assure you – never!"

"I like that!" Businessman nodded.

"Any more questions?"

A few mumbles of no could be heard.

"Okay then," Louisa continued. "Gentlemen, properly ask the lady to be your partner and ladies, properly respond."

The class completed putting into action what they had just learned.

Louisa then instructed the class to form two lines facing her, making sure the man placed the woman on his right side, hands in the correct position. "One of the most important things associated with the dance is your smile. It is very imperative, especially when competing to smile. Smiling indicates that you're in tuned with your partner."

"Don't wear a serious look on your face," Emilio added. "Smiling is part of interacting with your partner and it'll take you a long way in the competition."

"That's right!" Louisa concurred. "So get used to smiling. I want to see a lot of smiling here at The Ballroom." Louisa saw the serious expressions and repeated herself. "I said that I want to see a lot of smiling here at The Ballroom!"

The students broke into smiles, some chuckled.

"Emilio and I are going to teach you five basic steps in a moment but we want to make sure that you all understand something. We were told that this question was asked by just about all of you at the registration table.

"You will learn, here at The Ballroom, Detroit Club Style which is different from other places which is different from an international level."

"I was wondering about that," the guy sporting the Cartier's interjected.

"Detroit Club Style is the way Detroiters express their style of ballroom. Chicago has their way, so does D.C., Virginia, Baltimore – everywhere. The steps are influenced by styles such as, the Waltz, the Fox Trot, the Lindy Hop, the Swing but with a little twist."

"So we won't be learning steps used in international competitions?" another student asked.

"Right!" Louisa answered. "This competition is based off of amateur style rules, not international. International is an entirely different animal."

The lady with the Mohawk raised her hand and asked, "Just out of curiosity, do you know how to dance on that level, international I mean?"

Louisa smiled and nodded. "I do," she said humbly. "Any more questions?"

"I have a question," Jeff said, waving his hand. "You mentioned that the steps were influenced by other styles with a twist. Once we learn the dance, will we find ourselves adding our own twist?"

"Absolutely," Louisa and Emilio said at the same time.

"In fact," Louisa went on. "We better see your personality in the dance. Okay?"

"Okay," the class said with much excitement and enthusiasm.

"Any more questions? Does anyone want to bail out?"

"I don't," Businessman spoke up. "This in and of itself is unique."

The class agreed and excitement seemed to have heightened.

Louisa asked the D.J. to play the music and she and Emilio demonstrated five basic steps and then taught each one to the students.

Louisa led the class, "Step off on the right foot. Wait for the next beat and one, two, three, step back. One, two, three, step back, count it in your head. One, two, three, step back, one, two, three, step back."

The class was in sync, Louisa moved on. "Half turn, one, two, three, step back, one, two, three, step back. Send the lady out, one, two, three, step back and bring her back, spin her around, ladies on the balls of your feet."

Louisa had to stop them every so often so that she and Emilio could give further direction, to some more than others. "Brooke, you cannot lead this dance. The man is in total control. Let him lead you, let him guide you, go where he takes you."

Brooke nodded in agreement.

"Jade, this is The Ballroom, not Club Hip Hop, stop bouncing. Just walk, walk in beat with the music okay?"

Jade nodded in agreement.

She continued addressing the class. "We are going to learn this dance step by step but that could be a drawback because you'll tend to make the steps routine and they are not. Keep that in mind for the competition and for Friday and Saturday nights if you decide to come down to dance. Ladies, try not to assume your partner's next move, just follow his lead." She signaled to the D.J. "Select a faster tune, so they can pick up the pace and practice without direction."

The students practiced and Louisa sashayed to the spot where Jeff stood and tapped her foot, tightening the muscles in her legs. "Jeff, don't look at your feet, they won't leave you, your feet will go where you take them."

He nodded in agreement.

"Everybody! Always, eye level. And complete a step before you go into the next. Don't rush out of it or into it. If you miss a step, don't show it on your face, go smoothly back to the basic walk."

She gracefully twirled in front of Ivan. "Relax, Ivan. You're holding her hand too tightly and bending her wrist back. Hold her hand down, like this," she demonstrated. "Also, gently send her out, try not to push her too hard, she'll lose her balance. Got it?"

"Got it," he said feeling like he had been chastised.

"Okay class, take a break. If you don't know, the restrooms are just outside the main doors. The bar is open or you can stay on the floor and practice. The floor is open to all so feel free to dance with someone who already knows how to dance. Emilio and I will be available to assist you and we'll reconvene to finish out tonight's session."

The lighting in the lounge resembled the color of an ocean. Fully stocked and clean. The staff, dressed in navy, swiftly moved about catering to the guests. The long bar was equipped with backless stools and The Ballroom was inscribed on the overstuffed cushions. Brooke and Jade took the last two stools and Jeff and Ivan stood behind them, each ordering a drink. Corona with a lime for Brooke and for Jeff, a watermelon martini for Jade and Hennessey, straight for Ivan.

"I got it," Ivan told them, giving the bartender two twenty dollar bills and telling him to keep what was left.

Jade was impressed. "Big spender, eh?"

"Well you know," he said proudly.

Jeff and Brooke said thank you politely. Brooke continued, "I'm having a lot of fun. I can't wait to learn more."

"It is fun but very technical. It's not as easy as it looks," Jeff added.

"The only thing I don't care for is switching partners after each song," Brooke said.

"The purpose is so that you'll be able to go anywhere and dance with any guy," Jeff reminded her.

"I know," she said evenly. "It's just that I get used to one partner then I have to give him up and get used to another. I guess I don't mind the challenge though."

"Maybe the more we learn, the easier it'll be adapting to changing partners," Jade concluded.

"All Debbie Allen needs is her stick," Ivan hissed.

They were all quiet for a moment before Brooke decided to speak in her defense. "Louisa's tough, but it's obvious that she knows the dance. She's shown and proven that."

Ivan swallowed his shot and said, "Relax, Ivan. You're holding her hand too tightly. Gently send her out, try not to push her too hard, she'll lose her balance. Got it? I felt like she was talking to me like a child."

Jeff took a big gulp of beer and said, "She gave that kind of instruction to everyone in the class."

"Then everyone should feel the way that I do."

"As a personal trainer, I can tell you first hand that teachers have their own style." Jade began as she sipped her martini. "There are times when I have to push my students in order to get them to push themselves. We're not trying to be their parent, we're trying to get them results and we can't always hold their hand, especially when you have ten or so other students to be concerned about."

Jeff and Brooke looked at Jade, surprised by her answer. "I wasn't offended when she told me to let my partner lead," Brooke said. "If she doesn't tell me what I'm doing wrong, how am I going to do it right? That's why we're here, to learn what she already knows."

"And don't get me started on Emilio," Ivan continued to rant. "What's all this proper way to ask a lady etiquette crap? What big difference does it make?"

Nobody cared to touch Ivan's last issue.

Changing the subject slightly, Jeff said, "Well Brooke, it seems that you're a woman who likes to be in control, what are you going to do about it?"

Brooke laughed and finished her drink. "What are you going to do about watching your feet? And you Jade–"

"I know, I know. Some of my aerobic steps have a lot of bounce in them. I guess I have to change my mind set." She flipped her hair and using Louisa's voice she said, "I better get that bounce out before Louisa sends me to Club Hip Hop."

"Not so much nasal in my voice," Louisa said from behind them. "Give me more throat."

Brooke, Jeff and Jade laughed but Ivan didn't. He turned his attention toward the dance floor. "Louisa, how long were you standing behind us?" Jade asked embarrassed.

"Just long enough to hear you talking about me behind my back."

"I'm sorry I was mimicking you." Jade said, finishing her drink. "Please don't send me to Club Hip Hop, I'm not ready for those dance moves."

Louisa touched Jade shoulders. "If you promise to get that bounce out."

"I will.

"Good!"

"And anyway Ms. Louisa, what do you know about Club Hip Hop?"

Louisa did a move and then another after seeing the surprised look on Jade's, Jeff's and Brooke's faces. "Ha! That's what I know about Club Hip Hop. My husband and I can do every dance known to mankind, not to toot my own horn…"

Jade made a sound of a horn.

They laughed.

"My husband teaches classes over there on Saturday mornings," Louisa continued. "And the next time any of you go, let me know and I'll have my son put you on his list."

"The infamous D.J. Tony Tone of Club Hip Hop is your son?" Brooke asked.

"Mistamonotone is my son. So remember, tell him his mother sent you."

"We will," Jeff said.

"Great! We know Jade has to get that bounce out but how are the lessons coming for the rest of you?"

"Great so far. I'm going to work on being a follower or rather, I'm going to work on letting the man lead the dance," Brooke answered.

"Very good. And you Jeff?"

"I'm going to see this thing to the end," he answered.

"Stick with it and you will." The group looked to Ivan whose disposition answered Louisa's question. "I'll see you guys back on the floor in a few, don't think about it, just do it."

Once the class was back on the dance floor and had finished practicing, Louisa gave them final instructions. "Ladies, reflect on your hands. Some of you keep them down. Keep them where the man can reach for them without having to find them. Men, reflect on your leadership skills. Can you lead a young lady in her daydreams? I hope to see each of you next week. Oh, and please, remember to smile, smile, smile."

The men followed the ladies back to the table to pick up their purses. Ivan told them, "Let's exchange business cards."

"That's a good idea," Jade agreed. "We could keep up with each other outside of class."

They exchanged cards, taking a moment to read each one.

"You mentioned earlier that you were a personal trainer but when I first saw you, I could tell that you're into health and fitness. You're well-toned," Brooke said to Jade.

"Thanks, Brooke but you're no slacker, girl. You have a great body. Do you work out?"

"Yes. I work out at Motor City Fitness Club. I try to hit the gym at least three times a week."

"That's great. I used to work at Motor City Fitness Club."

"Really? Why aren't you still there?"

"Well, it was a great ride but at the time I was just trying to get as much experience as I could, where I could and of course progress financially."

"Makes sense."

"Hey, you're more than welcome to join me at Fenton, anytime."

"I'll keep that in mind, thank you."

"By the way, I have to tell you that your hair color is very pretty."

"Thank you."

"Flashlights? Right?"

"Yes."

"Speaking of Fenton," Jeff said. "I graduated from there in the mid nineties."

"Oh, yeah!" Jade stated. "I graduated from Fenton too in the mid nineties. Brooke? Ivan?"

"Yep," Brooke answered proudly. "I am a Fenton graduate and it sounds like we graduated around the same time."

"What about you Ivan?" Jade asked.

He shoved his hands in his pockets and slightly frowned. "Nah, I'm not a Fenton graduate. College is overrated and it's a waste of time and money."

It was silent for a moment then Brooke said, "It's a wonder we never ran into each other while at Fenton."

"I agree," Jade responded. "But Fenton is a huge university."

"Brooke," Jeff interjected. "You're in law enforcement?"

"Yes."

"You must be the police or the FBI." Ivan added.

Brooke didn't respond. Instead, she said to Jeff, "Jeff Ryan, sports writer for the *Detroit Daily*?"

Jeff nodded.

"I read your articles all the time."

Jeff was intrigued and a little surprised. "Are you a sports fan?"

"I am indeed. Football is my favorite."

"A woman who loves football and drinks beer! I'm in love with you already," he said teasingly.

Brooke knew that he was teasing but her heart skipped a beat anyway.

"Do you have a favorite team?"

Brooke heard him talking but she didn't really hear what he was saying. She was still hanging on to him saying that he was in love with her already.

"Do you have a favorite team?" he asked again.

"Yes," she answered as if he had just asked her. "I have to say the Lions because I am a Detroiter and you just have to support the home team but I am a Chief's fan."

"I support our home team too but I like the Steelers and the Colts. Who's your favorite player?"

Jade flipped her hair and said to Jeff, "I like sports too, you know. Basketball is my favorite. My favorite players are Ripleton and Sean Phillips."

"Rip Hamilton and Chauncey Billups!" Brooke stated.

"Oh," Ivan stepped in. "I'm a season ticket holder, Pistons of course." Well, one of his lady friends was the ticket holder but he could get both tickets from her if Jade wanted to go to a game.

She looked at his card again. "That is so cool but when do you have time since you're manager of I. James Service Center?"

He waved his hand. "The owner's my brother, he cuts me slack all the time."

Putting the information together, she exclaimed, "Ian James is your brother? My sister takes her car there all the time."

Ivan nodded. "Yep, that's my brother. And I apologize. The cell number is good but not the title and the business telephone number. You see, it's an old card. Ian officially made me his business partner. We're opening another service center real soon."

"Wow," she said impressed. "Just how old are you?"

"Thirty-fiv – thirty-two."

"Hey, I'm thirty-two, too. Jeff, Brooke, how old are you guys?"

"Twenty-nine," Jeff answered.

Hesitantly, Brooke answered, "Thirty-one."

"Cool," Jade said and the exchange between she and Ivan continued. Mostly about the things Ivan said he owned.

Brooke turned to Jeff and said, "Listen, it was nice meeting you. I got to get out of here. I look forward to seeing you out on the floor next week."

"Same here," he said sincerely. "Hey, let me walk you to your car."

Ivan chimed in, "We're headed that way, we can walk out together."

As the foursome headed for the door, Brooke fell a few steps behind and discreetly tossed Ivan's card in a nearby trash can. He only received one point and that was for smelling like Ferragamo. Picking up the pace, she stepped out the door Jeff had held open for them. "Thank you," she said pleased at his gentlemen-like behavior. Out in the darkened night, the conversation almost rested on Ivan's possessions when Brooke interjected and asked what everyone had planned for the weekend. That confirmed that Jeff didn't have a date, which could mean that he may not be seeing anybody.

They just so happened to have parked several spaces away from each other, except for Ivan who made sure everybody knew that valet would be bringing his Corvette around. Jeff and Brooke continued their walk while Jade stayed behind with Ivan asking him about his sports car.

Jeff asked while opening her door after hearing it disarm, "You really asked me to be your partner?"

"I'm sorry. I shouldn't have mentioned it. I was only giving Emilio an honest answer."

"Don't be sorry," Jeff said. "I didn't hear you. When did you ask?" It was bothering him and he really wanted to know.

Right before Jade distracted you, she thought to say but didn't. Instead, she smiled and answered lightly, "Doesn't matter, I still got to be your partner."

He grinned. "Okay, but I really didn't hear you and again I say I'm sorry about that."

Brooke got into her car, left the door slightly open and started the ignition. Her music started playing loudly enough for Jeff to hear and at the same time, he saw a few CDs on the passenger seat.

"What is it, Jeff?" she asked, following his gaze, again, wondering what it rested on.

"I was noticing you– I mean, your CDs, Dave Koz, I have that same CD."

"I like it, do you?"

"It's all right. It's quite different from his work on *The Dance* and *Saxophonic*, for instance but he still plays his sax the way he should on each track."

"*It Might be You* is a beautiful song."

"It is," he said evenly, debating if he should tell her about him playing the saxophone.

"My favorite Dave Koz song of all time is *Right by Your Side*," she offered. "He dedicated it to his father on *The Dance*."

"I'm more of a Kirk Whalum and Richard Elliot fan though."

"I like their music, too including Boney James and Pieces of a Dream. Jazz is one of my favorites but I love all types of music from reggae to house to pop to hip-hop and R&B. How about you?"

"Same here. I like all types of music but I listen mostly to jazz. I may have the largest CD collection in the state, from Miles to Coltrane to Albright and Roberson."

"Sounds like a true jazz fan to me. I only like smooth jazz which my cousin, refers to as "fake" jazz."

"Fake jazz – eh?"

"That's what she calls it although she likes it too and respects all the smooth jazz musicians but like you, she likes "real" jazz."

He nodded leaving silence between them. Both had so much more to say but really didn't know where to begin.

"Well, I don't want to keep you," Brooke finally said. "See you next Thursday?"

"See you next Thursday," he said. "I'm closing your door," he warned before doing so. Giving her a final wave, he walked toward his own vehicle and climbed inside. Before Brooke drove off, she glanced in Jeff's direction and saw that he was looking in hers. His expression read curiosity but unfortunately she didn't know what the curiosity meant. He then smiled and motioned for her to drive off. She did with no one but Ingrid on her mind. She couldn't get to her cellular phone fast enough to call and tell her about Jeff Ryan and of course about her first night at The Ballroom.

~

Chapter Six

At The Ballroom, the foursome fell into a routine, stemming from their first night – meeting at their table, "shooting the breeze" before class, ordering their favorite drink during break while they talked about the steps that they had learned. Then, after class, seeing each other safely out of the parking lot.

Louisa and Emilio had taught them many steps over the next few weeks, such as, The Sweetheart, The Cuddle, The Reverse Cuddle, Man's Reverse, Man's Duck and Sweeping the Floor. However, the class was having trouble "closing up" and "opening up" that is, going into the basic walk from the two-step.

"Think of it this way," Emilio said, while demonstrating with Louisa. "The lady and the man, in rhythm are connected and then they separate to get into the dance."

Louisa had separated the men from the women on either side of the floor. She worked closely with the men while Emilio worked with the women. Of course, both genders were elated about the personal attention from the very "hot" instructors.

Jeff kept stealing glances at Brooke and Jade. He liked them both for different reasons and even more so when it was discovered that neither one was in a serious relationship. Brooke was attractive, had a great personality, character, style and carried herself well. She was smart and confident, poised. He was almost sure that they had a connection but he concluded that only time would tell. He'd also be able to uncover their commonalities, besides sports and music.

Brooke was observant, Jeff noticed and he sensed that she knew when to hold and when to fold. There was also something mysterious about her, which was definitely a plus. Jeff didn't know what that mystery was but he was considering trying to find out.

Jade was nice enough and so beautiful that it was hard not to stare at her. Jade was friendly and full of life. She seemed as if she didn't have a care in the world. She wasn't as polished as Brooke but appeared to be very confident – probably overly confident. In fact, this signaled some insecurities, in his opinion. Jade had a great career as a personal trainer and he was impressed by her knowledge of health and fitness. Although Jade was fickle, he still felt a need to see if there was more to her.

It was his turn to practice with Louisa that brought him back from his reverie. He followed her instruction concentrating on the dance. Peering over Louisa's shoulder, he looked at the ladies one last time and then zeroed in on Jade. He'd call her tomorrow and invite her to lunch.

Since Jeff and Jade both worked downtown, Jeff suggested that they meet at Salsa Thai. He had arrived before Jade and asked the hostess to seat him while he waited. Sipping on a Coke, he watched Jade emerge from her bright red car, sporting fitness gear and a matching jacket in the same color. The outfit complimented her every curve. She was flipping her hair and pretending not to notice drivers swerving, trying to avoid hitting each other while keeping an eye on Jade.

He met her at the door and along with the hostess, escorted her to their table. When the server approached, they ordered a couple of spring rolls, Pad Thai for him and Vegetable Kow Pad Pak and hot tea for her.

"Excellent choice," Jade said after the server walked away.

"Thanks. This is one of the many places my colleagues and I frequent."

"Oh?"

"Yeah."

"Where else do you go?"

"It may be easier to tell you where we haven't been. You know, there are plenty of places to eat downtown and we've been to just about all of them."

The server returned with Jade's tea and gave Jeff another Coke. While Jade prepared her tea, she said, "I don't get out too much so I brown bag it a lot because our sessions are back to back and sometimes students have questions or concerns that need my attention."

"How were you able to get away today?"

"Amber," she answered, sipping her tea. "She's a big help! We back each other up all the time so students never have to worry about not getting the help they need."

"Well, I'm glad that you were able to get away. Thanks for having lunch with me."

"No problem," she responded, flipping her hair and grinning. "What made you ask me anyway?"

Jeff gave her a quizzical look before responding. He wasn't quite sure why she asked that question. He shrugged and replied, "just thought it would be a good idea to have lunch with you, get to know you without having to yell over the music."

Not really satisfied with the answer, she said, "Well, men usually tell me that they asked me out because I'm gorgeous. I just *expected* you to say it, too."

Jeff stared at her blankly. He wasn't sure which way to go since he was so taken aback by her statement.

The server placed their dishes in front of them, made sure that they were satisfied and left. Jade picked up where she had left off. "You do agree with them, don't you Jeff?"

"Agree with what?" he asked, mixing the rice noodles, green onions, bean sprouts and crushed peanuts together.

"That I'm gorgeous!" she said mixing her food together as well.

He ate a spoonful of food to stall. Thinking about it, he finally said, "Jade, I'm not sure what your looks have to do with us having lunch."

"My looks are the reason why you asked me out. Admit it!"

"What's your favorite color? Red? You seem to wear it a lot and I couldn't help but notice that you drive a red car as well."

She let out a laugh. "That's what I guessed." The rest of the time, in between flipping her hair and eating her meal, Jade talked about herself. Jeff couldn't get a word in edgewise and eventually tuned her out, adding occasional "ohs" and "aahs" and "reallys" for the record. Jade's revelations continued until they savored their dessert – Thai Style Ice Cream for him and Lemon Tart with strawberry topping for her. She finally said, "I've been running my mouth about me, what about you? What's the most adventurous thing you've done as of late?"

"Well," Jeff began, surprised and a little baffled at her sudden shift in the conversation and demeanor. "Besides these ballroom lessons, I went to Cancun. Perhaps neither is adventurous by most people's standards but they were the first things to come to mind."

"Do tell!"

Jeff described how beautiful, serene and peaceful it was in Cancun. He told her that there wasn't enough time spent in the place to really appreciate it. Jeff needed to go again to redeem himself but he didn't tell her what happened. He did say, however, that he would highly recommend it to anybody.

"Sounds like a magical place," she said. "I must keep it in mind."

The waiter approached with their bill. "I'll take care of it," he told Jade.

"Thanks," she said putting her money back in her purse. "I appreciate it."

He settled the bill with the server, then stood and pulled out her chair. "Jade?"

"Yes," she asked stepping aside.

"I mean no disrespect when I say this," Jeff said trying to soften the blow if what he was about to say was taken the wrong way. "You are a beautiful woman and I know you like to hear it but you have to realize that there is more to you than that. I'm sure there is more going on beneath the surface."

Jade caught a glimpse of Jeff driving behind her as they both headed back to work. Jeff himself was a gorgeous man but way too refined for her taste. She saw that in the beginning but had to live up to her image, that is, being "wined" and "dined" by eligible bachelors who wanted to spend time with her.

Reaching for her cellular phone, she dialed Ivan's number. Now Ivan was a force to be reckoned with. Ivan was the epitome of sexiness, he was aggressive and direct, just the kind of man she liked. It was very clear that Ivan had his "act together" his presence spelled success and more importantly, he was interested in her and her beauty. He told her so every Thursday followed by telling her to let him know when she was ready for a real man. And although it was odd that he said it while looking across the room at Jeff, after this lunch date, she was ready to be with a real man. She just hoped Jeff didn't run back to The Ballroom blabbing his mouth about their totally innocent lunch date because Jade didn't want to ruin any chance there was with Ivan.

His voice mail came on and she left a message saying that the time had come. When Jade returned to the fitness center, she helped Amber with the last sessions then went into her office to read and respond to e-mails. Ivan had left a message on her office phone voice mail. He gave Jade his address and directions from the center, saying that he entertained in his home and would love to entertain her. He told her to come right after work and that he couldn't wait to see her. She listened to his message twice before saving it and smiled. She had plans but she cleared her calendar and penciled him in. To Ivan's house she goes.

Ivan instructed the concierge to send Jade up to his apartment as soon as she arrived. Meanwhile, he chilled a couple of bottles of Moet & Chandon champagne and turned on his sound system. Barefoot, he checked himself out in the mirror for the third time, making sure he looked good in his Tommy Hilfiger jeans and a white T-shirt.

Ivan was sitting on edge every day since they exchanged business cards. He was hoping she'd call. When a woman calls a man first, it was a sure sign that she was interested and could easily be molded. Especially a woman like Jade, very lively, unlike that stuck-up Brooke. Brooke probably played by the book and had a lot of "don't do this," and "don't do that" rules. It was probably easier to catch a cheetah than to get even a phone call from her. Plus, it was apparent to him that Brooke was only tolerating him and even if she halfway cared for him, there was no way a woman like her would give him anything he needed – Jade was the opposite, eager to fit in and eager to please.

He wasn't quite sure of Jade's worth and how it would benefit him but in time he would discover it and he'd be ready to take advantage of it. In the meantime, he'd bask in her beauty, it certainly made him look good having eye candy to see and to be seen with. Now Jeff would never have her. He knew there was a chance she'd choose that pretty boy but Jeff didn't have the trappings to make her stay. He'd show Jeff how it was done.

When he had opened the door for Jade, the first thing he did was pull her in an embrace and held on to her for a while. Letting her go, he kissed her forehead, took her jacket and hung it in the closet. Then, he showed her around his place. He was more than satisfied at the "ohs" and "aahs" he heard fall from her lips as he took her from room to room.

He led her back into the kitchen and opened one of the bottles of champagne. Filling her flute and then his with the bubbly contents, he gave her a toast to her beauty, of course. Jade giggled as she sipped the champagne. After re-filling their glasses, he sat her on the counter top and fed her white chocolate covered strawberries while he talked about her and how fortunate it was to have her under his roof.

She had suggested that they practice their ballroom steps in the living room but he thought that was silly. Instead, they sat on the sofa and he talked about how great and wonderful his life was and how hers would be the same if she hung in there for him and helped him. He told her that Ian was helping him open his own service center and that they projected that business was going to be so big that Ivan's going to be able to buy that yacht and helicopter he always wanted to buy.
  Sensing that he had gotten her in his corner, he pulled her close and reached for the remote control. Turning off the music, he turned on the television set and watched as her eyes widened in awe. Flipping through the movie channels, she wanted to watch *The Notebook* with Ryan Gosling and Rachel McAdams but he decided that they would watch *De Ja Vu* with Denzel Washington and Paula Patton. Still, Jade snuggled closer to Ivan and giggled. Jade decided that yes, she would hang in there with Ivan and help him get wherever he needed to go.

~

Chapter Seven

Michigan's crisp air was typical during the fall season but it didn't stop the students from showing up at The Ballroom for their lessons. Louisa did not disappoint them, working them hard and leading them along the way. "Lead the lady!" she pleaded with the men. "You have to lead her if you don't, she won't know where to go." She stood in front of Jeff, took his right hand and spun him around. "Turn her, don't let her turn herself." She walked down the aisle and pleaded with the women as well. "Ladies, let that man lead you and let him turn you, some of you are turning yourselves." She stood in front of Brooke, grabbed her right hand and spun Brooke then spun herself. "Feel the difference?"

Brooke nodded then turned Louisa and then herself. "I can feel the difference."

"Good! This is what we'll work on for the rest of the class, spins and turns. There is a difference but both have to be smooth or you won't make it through the step. I'll work with the ladies on spinning and turning.

"Emilio will work with the men on turning the lady and he'll also work with you guys on body language."

"Body language!" Ivan stated.

"Yes. It is your line of communication to your partner. You have to send her the right signal at the right time. Depending on the step, it could be a gentle push on her wrist or the small of her back.

"Understand, very few dancers talk their partner through the dance, if any. He relies on his body and hers."

"How can the lady get a better understanding of what kinds of things to feel for?" Jade asked.

"Good question Jade. Understand that every man dances differently and communicates differently and this is why we change partners so that you can get used to falling in sync with any dancer.

"To answer your question, as you learn the dance, you will learn communication but sometimes it comes naturally."

Emilio chimed in, "for example, when he sends you out, he'll place his hand on the small of your back and gently push you. That's letting you know that he wants you to step forward." Placing Jade in the proper position, he sent her forward and caught her hand. "Freeze," He said stopping her from moving. "Now, I am going to give you a gentle jerk and spin you." He did. "That forced you to spin. Feel it?"

"Yes," she answered.

"So as Louisa said, as you listen and learn, you will begin to discover how your body should feel. You'll see that in a moment during the spin class. Louisa will teach you how to use your arms for balance and how to anchor your feet."

"So, who's up for the challenge?" Louisa asked.

Everybody sighed, mumbled and grumbled but took their place on the floor.

Louisa nodded. "Good! And remember to smile, smile, smile. I want to see all thirty-two teeth from everyone in here."

During the break, Brooke had noticed a difference between Jade and Jeff but didn't quite know why there seemed to be a little tension. Ivan, though, was up to his old self, making it known that he and Jade were getting to know each other better, as he put it. That was the least of her worries. She had a good idea that she wanted to run past Jeff just as soon as she could get him out of ear shot of Ivan and Jade. Finally, the door opened.

"Hey Jeff, how about a dance before break ends."

He stared at her and suddenly felt flushed. Not saying a word, he took her hand and led her onto the floor.

The two laughed their way through a few steps before Jeff admitted that he needed more practice.

"I've got an idea," Brooke said as she tried desperately to follow Jeff's mixed signals.

"I'll listen if you promise to stop laughing at me."

Between laughs, she said, "I'll try."

Jeff looked down at his feet, concentrating a little too hard on the step.

"Jeff, don't look at your feet, they won't leave you, your feet will go where you take them," Brooke instructed him as if she was Louisa.

"What?" Jeff asked looking at her, catching her gaze which made his heart skip and he tried to ignore the feeling but failed miserably. "What?" he stumbled, trying to find his train of thought.

Brooke blushed.

"You had an idea," he managed to get out.

"Let's get together on a Friday or Saturday night to watch the dancers."

"All right, that's a good idea. We may be able to pick up some pointers."

"Or at least get some inspiration."

Messing up a step, he said, "I thought Louisa told you to let me lead!"

She let out a laugh. "Don't you even try it, you've been sending mixed signals all night."

Jeff stopped and looked at her. He couldn't help but wonder if she meant anything more than the dance. Was he sending her mixed signals? Was he looking way too much into her comment? It certainly made him think about his feelings, especially after lunch with Jade. He wondered if Brooke knew about it and if he was unconsciously showing them both interest. And speaking of Jade, he had a feeling that she didn't want him to mention lunch to the group, otherwise, she would have made it a point to bring it up herself. Now he saw why she had chosen Ivan. He wasn't surprised.

Seeing his expression change, she asked, "What is it Jeff?"

He shook his head and led her in the basic walk.

She worried for a moment. She had hoped it wasn't anything she said. The last comment was about him sending mixed signals. She had hoped that he knew she wasn't trying to be factious. Maybe it was something else. She'd talk to Ingrid about it later and get her perspective.

"When would you like to start coming to watch the others?"

Just snapping out of her thoughts, she said, "Pardon me?"

"I asked when would you like to start coming to watch the others?"

"If you take me out of the basic walk, I'll tell you."

Jeff snickered and led her to spin.

"How about this weekend? Friday, Saturday!"

He led her into the reverse cuddle. "I have plans on Friday but Saturday is good."

"Okay. We should get here early so that we can get close to the dance floor."

"Nine-thirty, ten o'clock?"

"Nine-thirtyish."

He led her into the cuddle. "I can pick you up or we can meet here, whatever you're comfortable with."

"I'll meet you here," she answered trying not to faint. Ingrid better be awake for tonight's call.

Brooke circled the parking lot at The Ballroom in search of Jeff's car. Finding it would give her time to make her heart stop racing. If he hadn't arrived, she'd have ten minutes maybe, if he had arrived, five minutes – tops. She was on pins and needles the entire drive, playing over in her mind how to behave. Brooke had hoped cool and calm. That's how Brooke would be if she didn't have "feelings" for him but everybody knew it doesn't work like that. Once you enter the stage of "feelings" you got the butterflies and they never went away. In fact, they always seemed to come when you least expected it. She was just glad Jeff couldn't see the butterflies.

Brooke also wondered how Jeff felt about her because she sensed that he was weighing his options between her and Jade and couldn't blame him. She had weighed her options, too. There were a few others, like businessman, whom she had considered getting to know. None had even come close to Jeff. Ivan was definitely out of the question. She'd seen Ivan's kind time and time again but couldn't quite pinpoint his story. However, she knew that something wasn't right about him. And just like Jade, something was very superficial about him.

She spotted Jeff's car and then saw someone pulling out of the spot next to his. Perfect! She waited for the person to drive off before pulling into the space. If Jeff was still weighing his options, she just needed some time to influence his decision. Getting out of the car, she started for The Ballroom.

As soon as Brooke stepped inside the blue, plush lobby, she started looking around for Jeff. She walked by the water fountains when she felt a hand slide across her waist. She got a whiff of his Issey Miyake and knew it was Jeff. She smiled and immediately fell into his embrace, holding him longer than normal. Now was the time for her to drop her books in front of him and she hoped he'd pick them up. He escorted Brooke to coat check, helped her with her coat and paid the attendant.

Finding a table as close to the dance floor as they could possibly get, Jeff pulled out Brooke's chair and waited for her to get settled before taking the chair next to hers. She settled in even more. They both saw Louisa on the dance floor dancing with a man who must have been her husband; the chemistry was such that he had to have been. Louisa too finally saw them and waved as she continued to dance in step on the already crowded dance floor.

They continued to watch as the waiter approached, took their order and returned with spinach dip, toasted baguette slices and raspberry lemonade.

"Have you ever been to Skye's?" Jeff asked passing her a plate, napkins and a fork.

Brooke shook her head, "No but I hear the food is excellent?" Placing a napkin over her lap, she asked, "Have you been there?"

"No but as with you, I've heard that the food was excellent. Maybe we should, I mean could check it out." He pushed the dish of spinach dip in front of her. "Ladies first."

"Thanks," she said spreading her dip on two baguette slices. "And checking out Skye's one day sounds like a good idea to me. I love seafood."

"You and I like some of the same things," Jeff commented as he spread the dip on two baguette slices.

"Seems that way. We both like sports, food, music and our family values seem to be similar."

"Really, how so?"

"I don't know, from what you told me, your parents remind me a lot of my parents as far as how they raised us and their outlook on life. You seem to be big on family and so do I. It must be so cool having siblings."

Helping himself to more dip, he responded, "Sometimes, in fact, most times but there are times I could do without them."

"When are those times?"

"When they annoy me. You don't have to worry about that being an only child."

Brooke helped herself to more dip but not before Jeff noticed her expression changed to somber. She caught herself and looked up at Jeff. "Yeah but I guess it would be still be cool having a sibling." Pumping herself back up she said, "Ingrid is like a sister though."

"Is Ingrid your best friend, the one who told you about the lessons?"

"Yes, she is. Good memory!"

"I am a reporter, you know!"

"Is Jeff Ryan being cocky?"

"No Officer Carrington, I'm not!"

Brooke grinned. "How'd you know and don't you dare credit it to being a reporter."

"You confirmed it when you didn't answer Ivan."

Brooke picked up a napkin and wiped her hands clean. "You're very observant."

"Just as observant as you are."

She pulled a card out of her handbag and gave it to Jeff. "Here is my official business card. I use the one I gave you guys more often than not. Call me overly cautious but I reveal things about myself when I'm comfortable."

"Why not mention what you do up front?"

"I see a lot to make me more guarded than the average person," she said simply.

"I'd like to hear more – when you're comfortable, of course."

"Of course," she said drinking her lemonade.

"Can I call you dangerous girl?"

"Can I call you nosey boy?"

Jeff laughed. "You consider reporters nosey?"

"One of the nosiest professions in the U.S. of A. Always in somebody's business."

"Always in somebody's business," he mimicked her.

She giggled and changed the subject slightly. "Speaking of Ivan, he didn't exactly ask me what I did, he made a statement, which he always does and they're mostly side ways comments."

"To say the least. You don't care for the guy do you?"

Brooke shrugged her shoulders.

"I tolerate him," Jeff offered. "He seems to be crazy about Jade."

"So were you!" she said feeling him out only to see if there was anything "more" to him and Jade and to see if he would reveal any information about them.

"What?" Jeff asked only to make sure that he heard what she said.

"So were you!" she repeated, not making it easy for him.

"So was I what?" He was now buying time to collect his thoughts. He felt compelled to tread lightly but he wanted to be honest with her at the same time.

"Crazy about Jade. I'm observant, remember?"

"I'm not crazy about Jade, never was. Jade is who she is but she is a very nice girl."

"All right," she said pleased with his response.

"Let's talk about the competition, like what to wear and our music."

"What to wear? How about black?"

"Black?"

"Yeah. Black is elegant and classy and a tad bit sexy and Ingrid and I have already started shopping."

"I'm not surprised," he responded. "I do have sisters. And let me guess, the two of you saw something that I may like as well."

"Okay, busted again," Brooke answered in between laughs. "But at least we didn't buy it. We want you to look at it first."

"Thanks for thinking of me," he said teasingly. "Describe the prospective outfits."

"My dress is long with splits on both sides, speckled with stones and the bodice is sleeveless. And your outfit is basic pants and shirt," she said quickly.

He raised an eyebrow. "Well I have to see this *basic* pants and shirt. I may just have to settle for a suit," he concluded. "Music?"

"How about a mix of R&B, Jazz, Pop, Rap and Latin."

"We could start off slow, then speed it up, then slow it down."

Brooke nodded.

"Let's see if the D.J. will help us put our music together!"

"Think he'll do it?"

"It's either yea or nay."

"You're right!"

Jeff watched the dancers for a moment then he said to Brooke, "I don't know if I'll ever be that good."

"Aah come on, Jeff, just have fun. Learn as much as you can and have fun at the same time."

"If I don't get that good soon, I'm leaving and never coming back," he said jokingly.

"Don't go. Let me be an incentive to make you stay." She smiled but his smile was wider and he wouldn't take his eyes off of her. She coyly looked away and looked back only to see him still staring before he realized it and dropped his eyes but not before she saw him blush. Brooke was beyond herself. She had to admit that this was the first time she had ever seen a man blush over her. Sure, she got second looks, pleasant hellos and a wink or two but never a blush that anyone could have seen from the other side of the room. She reached up, thinking she should touch his face, but pulled her hand back subtly, so she thought.

He noticed but kept it to himself. "I'm not leaving," he finally said. "Not in a million years."

They watched the dancers in silence, stealing occasional glances at each other while making comments about the dance steps. She could get used to this. And if she played her hand right and if he played his right, there would be a next time. Jeff had picked up all her books tonight. Ingrid better be awake for tonight's call.

Jeff and Brooke had soon become regular visitors at The Ballroom on Saturday nights but had yet to practice what they learned on Thursdays. Both were using the excuse that they lacked talent but really they were just enjoying each other's company. They'd settled into watching the dancers and had tried every appetizer on the menu. Much to Brooke's delight, she could see in Jeff's eyes and tell by his body language that he was entering into another level with her. Brooke wanted to see it, needed to see it and she knew that something different was going to occur between them. And it had when Jeff had helped her with her coat and walked her to her car,

"I'd like to take you out sometime," he said simply. "And I know just the place I'd like to take you."

~

Chapter Eight

Jeff sat in his car in the parking structure of his high rise. He was ahead of schedule. His anticipation to spend the evening with Brooke was pushing him quickly to the next moment. He had his haircut, washed his car, showered and brushed his teeth twice. He even debated wearing his seat belt. Jeff didn't want to wrinkle his clothes, which he had ironed twice. After much fuss over himself, he rolled out of his parking spot. Better late than never.

Thirty minutes later, he had driven into Brooke's subdivision noting how the area was heavily wooded with lots of green, gold, brown and orange leaves on the trees painting a perfect fall scene. There were children out playing in the mild elements as the neighbors busied themselves looking after them or talking one to the other. Jeff realized he must have taken a wrong turn but it was okay. He was enjoying the scenery and had a few minutes to spare. Double-checking the address

Brooke had given him just hours before, he found her house within minutes.

Jeff sucked in a breath and rang the doorbell. Brooke opened the door and invited him inside. She was breathtaking, dressed in cream-colored dressy pantsuit. Her curls were pinned on top of her head, showing off a beautiful cream broach and matching earrings. She also sported matching bracelets. "You look ravishing," Jeff finally said not realizing that he had still been holding his breath. "And these are for you." He sighed while handing her a dozen pink and white roses.

Brooke's eyes widened. Receiving the roses in her outstretched hands, Brooke took them and embraced him. "Thank you very much. These are very beautiful." She stepped back, took a long look at him then took a deep breath. Although simply dressed in a pair of dress slacks, shirt and vest, he was well put together. "And you Mr. Ryan look ravishing yourself."

She started walking down the foyer with Jeff in step but he stopped and admired the fish aquarium mounted on the wall. "What's all in here?" he asked, causing her to stop.

Brooke walked over to the aquarium, standing very close to him, pointing as she explained. "There's Lonny Lobster and his wife Lonita. There's Franklin Frog and his wife Francesa. There's Demetrius Dempsy and his wife Demetria along with the Dempsy family.

"And there's the Green Terror family, they are very territorial but somehow they get along with the others. And there's the Snelly Snail family, they work with the algae to keep the aquarium clean."

He looked at her and asked, "You named them? You really know who's who?"

She met his gaze and then looked back at the aquarium. "Nope. I make them up as I go along but don't tell my dad, he really does know them by name."

"I take it this is your dad's aquarium?"

"Yes and there is more. Although this is the only aquarium mounted on the wall, my father has aquariums throughout the house. The sharks live in the library, the piranhas live in the basement.

"Silver Dollar and Goldfish live in the sitting room. South American Red Tail Catfish live in my parent's bedroom. And the beta fish, I only have one, named Small Blue, lives in my room."

"Can I meet Small Blue?"

She giggled. "Nice try. You can meet the sharks and the piranhas."

"Does your father take care of all the fish?"

She escorted Jeff into the living room. "Please sit down," she motioned for him to sit in one of the overstuffed chairs. "Yes, he feeds them, except for Small Blue but he has someone come in to clean all the tanks."

She noticed Jeff's attention turned to the photos on the fireplace mantel just as her parents walked in. When Jeff looked toward them, she removed a few of the photos and discreetly placed them in the drawer of one of the end tables.

Jeff Ryan, the friend, stood and approached her parents but not before Jeff Ryan, the reporter, noticed Brooke hiding the photos. He made a mental note not to ask her about it. It was obvious she didn't want him to see somebody and maybe time would reveal who that somebody was. Still, he noticed the strong resemblance between Brooke and her father but she was the opposite of her petite mother whose hair was styled and colored like Brooke's. "Hello, Mr. and Mrs. Carrington."

"Mom, Dad, this is Jeff, I've been telling you about him," she said proudly.

Her father shook Jeff's extended hand first. "It's a pleasure meeting you, Jeff."

Her mother shook Jeff's hand next. "Yes, it is indeed Jeff because we've heard a lot of great things about you."

"Thank you ma'am. I heard a lot of wonderful things about you and Mr. Carrington as well."

"How are the lessons coming?" her father asked him.

"They are coming along just fine. Brooke is very helpful in motivating me to stick it out."

"Well, David and I will be at the competition and we look forward to seeing you guys compete."

"Do you and Mr. Carrington ballroom?"

"Occasionally," her mother answered. "Especially when we go to events like the one David and I are headed to tonight. That's why we're dressed in formal attire. We're going to the Motor City Colors at The Art Museum of Detroit and there will be lots of dancing."

"Well, have a great time," he said.

"Are you rushing us off?" her father asked, really teasing Jeff.

"No sir, just very nervous," Jeff answered honestly.

"Reporters don't get nervous," Mr. Carrington commented, not letting up.

"Only when they meet the parents," Jeff said, not sure if he should laugh.

Brooke's father laughed so Jeff laughed. "How do you like your job, Jeff? I read your articles all the time."

"Thank you. It has its ups and downs but I have no real complaints. I enjoy writing, always have. And I've always followed sports."

"Your folks? What do they do for a living?"

"My mother is an interior designer for Homes Across Southeast Michigan and my father is CFO at Michigan Health Care Association. And my sisters own Classic Hair Designs."

"Is Lynne Ryan your mother?" Mrs. Carrington asked but didn't wait for an answer. "I've seen her work in that magazine and it is absolutely outstanding, simply remarkable."

"Yes, ma'am, she is my mother and thank you for complimenting her work. You should see my parent's home."

"I bet it looks just like those homes featured in magazines," she said.

"It does."

"I believe I have seen your father at several functions over the years, some sponsored by MHCA."

"My folks are always hobnobbing, especially my father because of his job so you've probably met him."

Mr. Carrington pondered for a moment. "Yes, it's coming back to me, I remember meeting him several times. He was very professional and personable." He paused then continued. "I'd really like to talk more Jeff but we must be going. It was nice meeting you." He offered to shake Jeff's hand again.

"Likewise, sir," he responded sincerely.

Mrs. Carrington took the roses out of Brooke's hand, "I'm going to put these in my favorite vase and put them in your room young lady," she said, squeezing Brooke's chin.

"Thanks, Mom."

"You're welcome. In the meantime, take Jeff into the kitchen and let him try my crab dip," she said, while walking toward the kitchen.

Grabbing Jeff's hand, Brooke led him into the kitchen just as her mother was finishing arranging the roses. Her mother offered Jeff her free hand and left the kitchen.

"They like you," Brooke told him as she washed her hands.

"They do?" he asked, following suit before sitting on a stool at the breakfast bar eyeing the crab dip on the sterling silver tray.

Brooke sat on a stool across from Jeff. Picking up a cracker and a spreader, she spread the dip on the cracker. "Yep. Their interaction in just those few minutes told me everything."

Jeff simply nodded.

Brooke fed Jeff the cracker. Giving him a few moments to savor the taste, she stated, "Tell the truth."

"I like it," Jeff said to her. *I like you even more,* he said to himself.

The thirty-minute drive back downtown was well worth it for Jeff. He was enjoying his time with Brooke and she seemed to be enjoying him. They talked a little about everything, learning as much as they could about one another, like their ideas and opinions about life and certain issues. He was impressed with her relationship with her parents and she had told them how they always left her current issues of the *Apartment Guide*. Brooke admitted that she was comfortable and would continue to build her "empire" until she was good and ready to leave. Jeff couldn't blame her, he'd stay if he was her.

Finally, they made it in and out of the parking garage and into the Fox Theater. Finding their seats off the main aisle in the fourth row, they situated themselves and anticipated their long awaited evening of jazz with Dave Koz.

"I want to remind you that I am a jazz fan," he warned. "When the lights dim, I am officially in jazz heaven."

"What's your favorite instrument?" She asked as if they were in a fairytale.

"The saxophone. What's yours?" he asked in the same voice.

They laughed. "I love the beat of the drums. I wish I knew how to play but I don't. Do you play the sax?"

"Every day!"

Surprised by his answer, she asked, "You do?"

He nodded. "I play every day," he emphasized each word.

"Wow, I'd like to hear you play, Mr. Musician."

"And I'd like for you to hear it. What good is music if you don't share it with anyone? If my father hadn't shared his love for the sax with me, I would not have known to love it, learn it and play it," Jeff said proudly.

The lights went down, the hostess started the show and Jeff proved himself to Brooke for the next forty-five minutes. He was in jazz heaven but she was there too, energetically moving with rhythm to Koz's sounds.

At intermission, they went into the lobby to stretch. While they waited in line to purchase water, they struck up a conversation with a couple about Koz's performance. Soon, the house lights flashed and they made their way back to their seats. The lights went down again, the curtain raised and Koz, with all his energy, took center stage. Halfway through the show, Jeff had taken the aisle with Koz himself, dancing to the piercing sound of the sax – while playing his imaginary sax, which encouraged the crowd.

After the concert, they walked next door to The Pasta Place and ordered a New York Style gourmet pizza. They ate and talked for so long, they closed down the place. Jeff wanted to tell her that this was one of the best days of his life but didn't want to tell her too much, wondering if he had already. He hoped it wouldn't be the last date and if there was another date, he hoped it was soon.

Jeff pulled in front of Brooke's home. He told himself he would call her again. Jeff also told himself that the end of this night was the beginning of a special relationship. He helped Brooke out of the car and walked her to the door. Jeff didn't expect an invitation into her home and was shocked when she extended it. It was late so he made her promise a rain check. She agreed and that confirmed a second date was coming.

Holding tightly to her hands, which seemed to have been nervously pasted at her sides, Jeff told Brooke that he had a good time and thanked her for a wonderful evening. She graciously accepted his thanks, expressing her gratitude as well.

"You will call when you get home?" she asked.

"I will."

He looked deep into her eyes then hugged her tightly. She pulled back first but he wasn't ready to let her go, not yet. She obliged.

As Jeff drove back home, he had begun to think. He could count the number of dates and he'd had plenty in all his dating years. None as good as his date with Brooke. She was different from all other dates. She let him open doors, slide out her chair, court her, participate in a conversation. Brooke didn't go along to get along and didn't ask him to take her out again. She didn't take up time trying to impress him. She was always a lady and knew how to be treated like one.

Jeff truly couldn't wait to see Brooke again. He knew pace and timing were very important. He remembered what his father told him, when opportunities like this knock, let them evolve. Opportunity was knocking and so was his heart. He admitted to being smitten by her beauty but more by her grace. Brooke was everywhere – in his thoughts, on his clothes and in his car. Her perfume, it just lingered, just like his longing for her and he loved it.

Jeff had barely entered into his apartment when he called Brooke.

"You made it home safely," she stated.

"I made it home safely," he replied. "What are you doing?" he asked.

"Waiting for your call," Brooke answered, as a giggle came out that she wished hadn't. "And watching a little TV," she added.

Jeff was flattered by her first response. He asked, "Anything interesting on?"

She pressed the mute button on her remote control. "Nah. Infomercials."

They were comfortably silent.

He spoke again, "Did I mention I had a good time?"

Her heart sank deep inside her chest and she warmed. "You did. I had a very nice time, too!"

More silence.

Jeff finally spoke, "Well, I better not hold you any longer, you must be tired."

Brooke paused. She was nowhere near tired of talking to him and debated whether to tell him but decided against it. "It is getting late."

"Good night."

"Good night."

Brooke hung up but Jeff held the telephone close to his ear, not quite ready to hang up – not just yet. *I've never had my breath taken away by a woman like you.* He said to himself just as his thumping heart drowned out the piercing sound of the dial tone.

The following Saturday, instead of just watching the dancers, Jeff treated Brooke to dinner at Skye's. Dining in the restaurant was like dining by the sea, as Skye's color scheme was sky-blue. The hostess, dressed in sky-blue, escorted Jeff and Brooke to a table for two by the windows so that they could watch the dancers. Over Surf and Turf, they made plans to return to Skye's on New Year's Eve, in just a few weeks and then spend the wee hours of the morning dancing at The Ballroom. They also talked about traveling, the places they'd been and the places they wanted to go. He had told her about his trip to Cancun and how it was a wonderful, beautiful place to visit. He had also told her about Robby and the almost arrest. Jeff admitted that he hadn't spoken to him since the incident and was wondering what happened to him but hadn't taken the time to call. A part of him felt that Robby would call if and when he was ready.

Jeff had wanted to make good on his promise and play the saxophone for Brooke. She was thrilled. He had invited her to his home since it was just a few miles down the street. She had become very hesitant and Jeff could sense her uneasiness. He tried putting her mind at ease and after a little convincing, she agreed and hoped it wasn't against her better judgment.

As they rode the elevator up to his apartment, Jeff checked for her expression. She was still a little tense. He gently rubbed her shoulder. "I don't bite," he told her jokingly.

"You could be a kidnapper," she shot back in the same tone.

He placed his hand on her hip. "I should be scared of you, you're the one with the handgun."

Brooke playfully pushed his hand away. "You're right but I can't go around shooting bad dates," she responded in between laughs.

As the elevator stopped on his floor and they entered into his apartment, he asked her if she'd like a bottle of beer.

"No," she said. "I have to have all of my faculties just in case I do have to put one in you."

They laughed.

Jeff lit the fireplace. While she poured them each a glass of beer, he retrieved his saxophone and started setting it up. Within moments, Brooke joined Jeff, sitting across from him in front of the fireplace. They talked a while, long enough to finish their drinks.

Standing up, he set his glass on the coffee table and picked up his instrument. Then, stood in front of her. He played a note, "This one is especially for Brooke Carrington." He played another note, "And I'd like for you to make a request." He played a melody.

She set her glass on the coffee table and forced the lump out of her throat. *"It Might be You!"*

He played another melody before he repeated, *"It Might be You!"* His starry eyes locked with hers and became fixed. He placed his lips on his mouthpiece and began to play as if it would be his last time. Their eyes never dropped.

When he played his last note, Brooke was speechless. She closed her eyes momentarily and opened them. She smiled. "That was beautiful."

He returned the smile. "Thanks."

She stood up and walked toward him. She hugged him tightly. "I wish that we could stay like this for a little while."

"What?" he asked hearing her but for some reason needing her to say it again so that he could hear it again.

She didn't respond.

"What?" he asked again.

She still hadn't repeated what she said.

He pulled back from Brooke's embrace and leaned his ear toward her to catch the response, "What?"

She kissed him softly. Hours went by before the kiss ended.

Jeff opened the door to his parent's home. He called out to them but they didn't answer. Holding the door open for Brooke, he invited her inside and escorted her into the living room. Brooke focused her attention on the photos of the Ryan family. The resemblances between Jeff and his sisters was striking, a combination of both parents.

"Why do you still have a key to this house?" A voice from the hall asked.

"Dad," Jeff responded, startled.

He approached Brooke and extended his hand. "And your lovely accomplice must be the much talked about Brooke Carrington!"

She gripped his hand and firmly shook it. "Nice to meet you, Mr. Ryan."

"You offer a bone-shattering handshake, that tells a lot about your character."

"Thank You."

He wrapped his hands around Jeff and pulled him close. Skillfully pulling keys from his son's back pocket, he dangled them in front of him. "Dad needs his keys, Jeff. You may ring the bell like all of our other guests."

They laughed.

"Where's Mom?" Jeff asked.

"Where else?"

"In the kitchen," they said in unison.

As they started for the kitchen, Jeff's father commented to Brooke. "I've heard many good things about you. My son is glad to have met you. He tells me you are lovely."

"And you have a lovely son. Fruit doesn't fall far from the tree."

"You're making a good impression, young lady," he said. "Let's meet the other lovely side of us. She loves to cook and spends most of her time in here."

"Hi, Mom," Jeff said as they entered the kitchen. His mother was just closing the refrigerator door. When she looked up and headed toward them, he continued proudly. "Mom, this is Brooke."

His mother shook Brooke's hand and motioned for her to sit at the table. Jeff pushed in her chair, then his mother's chair. Jeff and his father sat down to join the ladies. "It's a pleasure meeting you, Brooke, we've heard a lot of great things about you."

"Thank you, ma'am. I've heard a lot of wonderful things about you and Mr. Ryan as well. You remind me a lot of my own parents."

"That's a nice compliment," Mr. Ryan said. "I've followed your parents work in law over the years and I've always been impressed with their fairness. I've even had the pleasure of meeting your father on various occasions. He's very professional and personable."

"Thank you," Brooke said. "When my parents met Jeff, my dad mentioned that he had met you. Dad had similar sentiments about you, too. And Mrs. Ryan, my mother is in love with your work and judging by your home, she would fall in love with it as well."

"Well, send my appreciation to your mother, perhaps I can invite her and your father over one day."

"Perhaps," Brooke said hopefully.

"How are the lessons coming?" his father asked her.

"The lessons are coming along just fine. It's not as easy as it looks. It takes a lot of practice but I am looking forward to the competition."

"Well, Lynne and I will be at the competition and we look forward to seeing you both compete," Mrs. Ryan said.

"Do you and Mr. Ryan ballroom?"

"No." his mother answered. "We can handle the two step but never quite mastered the ballroom. Hey, maybe we'll sign up for lessons next year."

"When my wife and I heard you were coming, Lynne wanted to cook you something special so we asked Jeff what was your favorite food."

"And Jeff told us that every food is your favorite food," Mrs. Ryan added.

Brooke lightly pushed their son before calling out, "Jeff!"

He tenderly pulled her in an embrace. "You do like a lot of different kinds of food, sweetheart but you look so good because you can eat anything and work it all off."

"If you're trying to clean it up, you've just gone from bad to worse." She hugged Jeff back and let him go.

"So since we couldn't get a straight answer from Jeff," his mother explained. "I made you spinach dip."

"Umm. I like spinach dip," she responded.

"Good. And when you come to visit next time, I'll have your favorite meal ready for you. How does that sound?"

"That sounds great, Mrs. Ryan. It's true I like a lot of things like pizza, steak, hamburgers, french fries but my favorite food is lasagna."

"Then lasagna it is next time. Meanwhile, I'll get everybody served now," she promised before excusing herself from the table.

"Why the police force?" Mr. Ryan asked.

"I've always wanted to be an officer. It's always been in me to serve and protect and I had the opportunity to fulfill my dream. That is, after finally convincing my parents. I think that was tougher than anything."

"I bet," Mr. Ryan responded.

"It's the kind of job you have to love doing and I do."

"What's next for you?"

"Management."

"Management? Very good!"

"Thanks. I've been preparing myself for it for some time now. It's just a matter of time."

"That's great. I wish you the best and if there is anything we can do, don't hesitate to let us know."

"Okay," she said. "Thank you."

Once Mrs. Ryan prepared the table, they talked a while with Brooke, a little about a lot of things. Jeff knew his parents liked Brooke and were very impressed with her. And he knew that if she was "in" with his parents, Bacari and Autumn would like her, too – especially Autumn because Brooke and Autumn were a lot alike. Jeff, of course, told her so. Brooke had to admit that she was glad that his folks were pleased with her. She was pleased with them as well. And yes, he could be assured that Ingrid already approved of him.

~

Chapter Nine

Louisa and Emilio assigned the students to work with their competition partners for the remaining sessions. This particular session, they would learn and practice theatrical movements such as drags, dips, lifts, drops and leans. And of course smiling was reinforced.

Jeff had invited his sisters to The Ballroom, not only to see him in action but to also meet Brooke. Brooke had invited Ingrid to check out Jeff. The exchange between all of them was pleasant. Each had heard so many positive things about the other; everyone seemed to interact as if they had known each other for years. Autumn, Bacari and Ingrid had been told about Jade's personality but they accepted her. Besides, Jade was nice enough, very friendly and warm. Ivan was of course being Ivan but Jeff's sisters were neutral toward him. However, Ingrid and Ivan had a non-verbal square off over a handshake. Ivan accused her of being just like Brooke. Ingrid told him that she was worse than Brooke.

At the break, Jade told Jeff that she felt left out and was going to call Amber so that everyone could meet her sister. He just shrugged his shoulders and took Ingrid out on the dance floor – against her wishes – to see if she really had two left feet. She did but the interaction gave the two of them the chance to talk while Brooke had a chance to chat with Bacari and Autumn.

Funny thing, when the class started back up, Jeff noticed a well-dressed, very sophisticated older woman come in and brought it to Brooke's attention. It was her grandmother. Completely surprised, she pulled Jeff off of the dance floor and introduced him and his sisters to her grandmother. Then, she scolded her grandmother for being out "late" and for being at The Ballroom.

Her grandmother explained that she saw Ingrid at the supermarket. And after Ingrid told her about tonight, she decided to come because she wanted to meet Jeff as well. Brooke looked at Ingrid and Ingrid vowed that she had no idea that her grandmother was coming.

Jade and Ivan made their way over and they all listened to Brooke's grandmother tell them about her days as a dancer. They all instantly fell in love with her. She was simply a sweet old lady. Even Ivan thought she was pretty cool. Brooke and Jeff told Louisa that they were going to leave class early to make sure Brooke's grandmother had made it home safely. Autumn, Bacari and Ingrid were right behind them, promising to hang out again, of course before the competition.

They were all walking out just as Amber showed up. The introductions were brief and Jade was disappointed.

~

Chapter Ten

Things had changed over the course of weeks, not much attention had been placed on Jade and she was beginning to feel like she was losing her touch. The only one giving her attention at The Ballroom was Ivan, but even she had to admit that it was only on his terms. As much time as they spent together, they had never been outside of his home or hers – not a theater, not a movie, not a dinner, not a trip down the street, well maybe down the street to the pizza place and Blockbuster then back to her place or his. She'd asked him many times for a real date but Ivan insisted that dates were overrated and that he enjoyed having her all to himself – just the two of them.

   She truly wanted something that Jeff and Brooke had. The chemistry between them was unbelievable. The couple shared with her places they had been and things they had seen. She couldn't help but to wonder if she had made a mistake. Jeff had chosen her first, hadn't he? What went wrong? What did she say or didn't she say? What did Brooke have that she didn't? Jade had Jeff right at her fingertips first. He was supposed to stay interested and chase her, Ivan or not. As much as she secretly wished Ivan were like Jeff, Ivan had an indescribable kind of power over her. It was magnetic, kind of hypnotic.

New Year's Eve, one of the most important times of the year apparently wasn't all that important to Ivan. Soon after they heard about Jeff and Brooke's plans, Ivan had called Jade with plans of his own. This was supposed to be their first official, unofficial date. They'd have dinner at Skye's then spend the wee hours of the morning dancing at The Ballroom just as Jeff and Brooke had planned to do.

Ivan promised to make the reservations and told Jade to just dress up in the prettiest dress she owned and to be ready at nine o'clock p.m. She had spent the entire snowy day getting ready. Seemingly countless hours at the beauty salon were spent, having her hair styled and nails manicured. There were several more anxious hours spent at the boutique shopping for that perfect dress. At last, Jade spent a couple more hours at the spa trying to relax before racing home to spend more time getting dressed.

Nine o'clock became ten o'clock. She called Ivan five times on his cellular phone – the calls went directly to voice mail. She was worried that something had happened, an accident, something involving his brother or maybe he had gotten tied up at the service center. He couldn't have forgotten could he? He certainly wouldn't change his mind.

He had to have been on the way, he was simply running late.

Eleven o'clock.

Four more calls went unanswered. She glanced out the window then she started second-guessing herself. Had he told her to meet him? She frantically found the telephone number to The Ballroom, called and asked to be transferred to Skye's. When she was finally put through, she asked the maitre de if anyone from the James party had arrived. The maitre de told her that there was not a reservation for James. She flipped her hair and asked him to verify that again.

Again, no reservation.

She flipped her hair and had asked him to verify if the reservation was under Stone.

Still, no reservation.

Eleven-thirty.

Jade called Ivan's cellular again while looking out the window.

Eleven forty-five.

Dressed in her best, she went outside and stood on the porch.

Eleven-fifty.

She looked in both directions. Snow had begun to fall. Jade checked her cellular phone's display and her voice mail. At eleven fifty-five, Jade knew the final countdown to midnight was in the final phase – "five, four, three, two, one!" In what seemed like seconds later, she heard gunfire in the distance, plus horns honking and few faint "Happy New Year" shouts. Flipping her hair, she went into the house and closed the door behind her.

The tears would fall though. She was halfway certain that Ivan James had a good explanation. She washed her face, took off her clothes and showered. She had taken a Tylenol PM and waited to dose off. Jade finally did and that's why she hadn't heard her telephone ringing at first. When Jade finally answered, her neighbor told her that someone dropped a man off in front of her house thirty minutes ago. He was standing just outside her door; the neighbor was going to call the police. Jade went to the door and looked through the peephole, thanked the neighbor and told him not to call the police.

Jade opened the door and Ivan stumbled into the living room, falling on the floor in his custom made Italian suit sending his shiny cuff-links and a bottle of Moet & Chandon champagne across the carpet. Using all of her strength, she moved his dead weight aside so that she could close the door and lock it. He was trying to tell her something but his words were slurred beyond understanding. However, the smell of old alcohol and cigarette smoke was present, as was the make-up on his shirt. Squaring her shoulders, she went into the bathroom and took another Tylenol PM before returning to her bedroom, closing the door, getting back into bed and falling asleep.

When the medicine wore off, Jade found herself stirring. Waking up fully, she looked at the clock, it read: twelve o'clock. The sunlight shined through the curtains creating warmth that had absolutely no affect. She wondered if Ivan was still passed out on her floor where she'd left him. She was way too tired and drowsy to deal with him. What excuse could he have come up with? It was very apparent that he had spent New Year's Eve with someone else, but why? And why hadn't he had the decency to tell her? And the nerve of him to show up, not even able to stand on his own two feet – smelling like the night before.

Jade lay in bed a little while longer. She just wasn't ready to face Ivan. Deep in her heart, Jade knew that whatever he said would only negatively affect her for a moment and she hated herself for it. She knew that she would give in and forget that she was really beginning to hate Ivan and herself even more.

She listened for sounds and movement but hadn't heard a thing so she checked her messages. One came from Amber, the other from her parents, all wishing her a happy new year. A couple of hours had passed before she got out of bed.

The only light in her house was peering through the windows. Jade peeked inside each room as she walked past. No signs of Ivan, just the faint smell of old perfume, cologne, smoke and alcohol. The champagne bottle was still on the floor but Ivan and the cuff links were gone. She picked up the bottle and locked the front door. Next, she went into the kitchen and tossed the bottle in the trash can. Feeling a little queasy, she went into the bathroom but quickly grabbed her bearings when she saw a note on the sink. It read:

"I knew you'd come in here sooner or later. I'm disappointed that you didn't help me when I came over, I was sick. It's too long of a story to explain what happened. I know that you will forgive me.

You're not the type of person to stay mad - you're too sweet of a person. I look forward to seeing you on Thursday. We only have about three months before competition.
 P.S. Happy New Year! Ivan"
 Jade successfully blinked back the tears now forming in her eyes. Ivan was right! She wouldn't stay mad at him long although she wanted to. Once she'd stepped into The Ballroom, all would be forgotten. And sure enough, two months had passed and they fell right back into their routine as if New Year's Day did not occur. Ivan never spoke of it and neither did she.

The students at The Ballroom listened attentively as Louisa, again, went over the guidelines for the competition. It was now just several weeks away. Louisa also answered questions and gave advice on music, clothes, technique and style. She considered the rest of the session open to allow couples to practice. Most couples practiced step by step as opposed to putting combinations together as they didn't want others to see their routine before the competition.
 Each moment Jade could find, she used it probing Brooke. She was desperate to know her secret. She and Jeff looked extremely happy. He was very attentive – genuinely attentive – and anyone could tell how much he adored her. Jade could also tell that Brooke was holding out. She sensed that Brooke had an answer but wouldn't tell her. It's the same sense she got from Jeff when they had gone to lunch.

Nonetheless, after many different approaches, Brooke would simply say, "There is no secret. I'm true to myself."

"I'm true to myself," Jade had stated, hoping to get more. Jade knew she couldn't out right ask Brooke more about her thoughts.

"Then that's all that matters," Brooke had responded evenly.

Jade felt she had no choice but to give up. No one would understand her – never have, never will.

Winter and spring were having a battle of the sorts. It rained for a while, it snowed for a while, rained for a while then snowed for a while. It had been doing that all day and by the time Jade left The Ballroom, it hadn't let up. Instead, the temperature dropped, making the roads slick and visibility poor.

As Jade drove the freeway toward her side of town, she had replayed the last several months in her head – from her first day at The Ballroom – up until the present. It started off great; she thought that it was one of the best decisions in her life. Jade had met some great people, including Ivan. Maybe in just a little time, he'd come around and be the type of man Jeff appeared to be. What was going on? She was used to being in charge of men, not men in charge of her.

Jade flipped her hair and switched to the far left lane of the three lanes of travel, then turned on her windshield wipers. She'd have to find a way to change Ivan so that he would look at her just the way Jeff looked at Brooke. She adjusted the heat and turned up the radio, listening to a tune ordinarily playing at The Ballroom. It stopped snowing and raining so she picked up speed forgetting that the roads were still wet. She had been too consumed about the events at The Ballroom and how she used to have game. Jade had always "been on top," and at the center of attention.

She drove behind an old, raggedy truck transporting bricks that weren't properly covered or secured. Still, the truck driver was speeding and so was she, lost in her thoughts. Everybody always liked her, everybody always talked about how beautiful she was.

The truck's brake lights shined red. Jade pressed her brakes as hard and as far as she could but slid on a patch of ice. A brick flew from off of the truck, shattering the windshield. The vehicle was moving beyond her control and trying to regain control was useless.

Jade's car hydroplaned over the two lanes. She sucked in a breath and turned the steering wheel. The car slammed into the median on the passenger side. Jade then screamed as the airbag deployed and the seat belt adjusted, holding her tightly in place. The car then spun around and hydroplaned back across all three lanes – barely missing oncoming traffic – before slamming into the median head on.

Jade could taste blood and the residue of the airbag exploding, seeping into her mouth. It tasted like copper and acid or an aspirin that had been chewed. She gasped, the pain was excruciating. It was really painful in her face, she had felt the glass cut across it after the brick shattered the window. It suddenly dawned on her.

Her face!

Oh gosh, not her face – not her pretty little face! Jade tried to move so that she could see for herself but she was pinned between the airbag and seat belt.

Not her face, she'd rather be dead.

The pain in her face, the blood flowing like a fountain, she fell unconscious.

The last place Jade had wanted to find herself was at Fenton Elementary School. There she was on the playground all alone because none of the other children wanted to play with her. They said she was "funny looking." Unbelievably skinny and awkward, the children said that the Ugly Duckling story was about her but she'd never grow into a beautiful swan. Her green eyes, matted hair, overbite and gapped teeth only made her look like a Martian, the children would say and her last name was Stone because Madam Medusa was her mother.

While most of the girls were getting love notes from the boys asking them to check the box, yes, maybe or no, she was only dreaming about getting them. There was this one boy she liked a lot and she thought that he liked her too but he didn't. He only wanted to walk home from school with them so that he could hold hands with Amber. It worked but Amber had no idea about the teasing until the boy made a joke about Jade starring in the next ET movie.

Amber beat him up and the teasing on the playground stopped, at least for a little while.

"I need you Amber! You always make the hurt disappear," Jade said regaining consciousness. The smoke in front of her was thick. She gagged, trying to catch the breath caught in her already tightened throat. She felt as though she couldn't keep breathing anymore, she fell unconscious again.

Getting older hadn't changed her appearance; in fact, it only seemed to get worse thanks to the thick glasses she was forced to wear. Her parents kept telling her that she was beautiful and that in time, she would change because everyone went through an awkward stage and her stage was now. Funny how she never remembered Amber going through any awkward stages, she was always adorable, everybody said so.

Back at school, she remembered the teachers having to pair her up when the class had to work in groups. No one would pick her and if she was captain, no one wanted to be on her team. The teachers were always so kind to her and reprimanded the children who were caught teasing but that only made the repercussions worse during recess.

One day at recess, the coolest boy in school waved a stick in front of her and told her that she looked like she got hit with an ugly stick. She hung her head and asked God to forgive her for looking like she got hit with an ugly stick. When she looked up, she saw Amber beating him up with that same stick he said looked like Jade got hit with it.

"I know Amber, I've got to learn to stand up for myself. I'm better at it now, aren't I?" she said regaining consciousness. "Amber, you got suspended from school that day but the teasing stopped, at least for a while." Jade could smell smoke and gas or something like it, she wasn't sure. She could also smell the dampness in the air. "Remember when mommy dropped me off at school and I'd sneak out and run back home to be with you for those three days? There was no way I was going to school without you, not until I learned to stand up for myself." She felt herself slipping out again.

Gone were the thick glasses but she was still forced to wear glasses. It's too bad, people would say, that she had such a pretty color of eyes and that was the only thing cute on her. Her hair would be pretty too if her mother knew how to make it look like Amber's. Well, at least they used pretty and Jade in the same sentence. She finally got those much-needed braces. It was a good thing but new names came like, "metal mouth," "brace face," "train track." Amber was still fighting for her and she was still hiding behind Amber.

It was bad enough that students said that they couldn't believe that she and Amber were related but to hear adults make similar comments was just as bad. They'd always dote on Amber and say how she was as cute as a button. Then, as an after thought, say to Jade, "Oh, you're cute, too." Relatives would offer to take Amber places but not Jade but their parents wouldn't have any of that. If you did for one, you did for both.

Her parents went into overtime trying to boost her self esteem but for a while it seemed like a waste. So many sleepless nights, so many tears. Her mother took her to the hairdresser and finally learned how to manage her hair. She mostly wore it pulled back in a sleek ponytail but it was better than it had been.

The effects of the airbag exploding was causing Jade's eyes to burn. Coupled with the pain in her face and across her torso, she started praying that the pain would go away. Jade wished she could undo this day and start it all over. Jade wished she hadn't been driving so fast. "Amber, I should really resent you after all these years but I don't because you were my comfort, you were with me every step of the way, taking up for me when I couldn't do it. I waited a long time to look just like you and now I do. I'm glad you're my sister."

The first two years at Fenton High School were rough without Amber. It forced her to become a little quick with the tongue, her form of defense. Contacts were a blessing. All of a sudden, braces were cool. Jade's new challenges were her weight and clothes. Still skinny as ever, it was hard finding clothes that fit causing the outfits to just hang. It seemed like there wasn't enough safety pins in the world to make all the necessary adjustments.

Curvy, cute as a button Amber entered high school and made friends very fast. She even ended up befriending the most popular girls at school and they were upper classmen. The first time they invited Amber to a party was the last. Problem was, they made it clear that Jade just didn't make the cut and couldn't be a part of their crowd. Amber told them that if her sister couldn't come, neither could she. That night, Amber executed her plan.

Stuck in her bedroom for about four weekends in a row, she was ready to transform Jade. It was time to fight fire with fire. The day came when she styled Jade's hair into the latest style, making sure the new look showed off her eyes and those dimples. One of her classmate's mother was a seamstress. And although her classmate didn't have permission, she gave Amber all the "barrowed" tools she needed to alter all of Jade's clothes, giving "jazz" to each outfit. Also, without permission, Amber "barrowed" some of their mother's make-up applying just enough to bring out Jade's features.

Pushing Jade in front of the mirror, she silently prayed that Jade would love her new look. After several silent but intense moments, Jade smiled and cried, she loved her new look. Jade hugged her sister and thanked her for making her pretty. Amber told her that the rest was up to her. Jade heard her but really, she had revenge on her mind. With her new look, those who made her life torture would regret it.

Her new look finally got the attention of a fellow senior and they soon became known as a couple.

He'd pick her up for school and drop her off at home. He'd walk her to her classes and wait for her by her locker so that he could buy her lunch. They'd dress alike on Fridays and she was at every baseball game he played. He told her that she should be a model and she believed it. He told her to go with him to Fenton University and she agreed. Jade quickly got used to that – finally someone paying her attention and giving her good advice at the same time. And the other boys started noticing her, too. She finally experienced being beautiful and she was never going back – never!

Jade could hear voices, people asking her if she was all right and asking her for her name. They were asking her if she was in pain and telling her not to move. They told her that help was on the way.

College was the best time of her life. It seemed like the night before her first day, she drank a glass of milk. When she woke up the next morning, she had the curves she'd spent years dreaming about. The swan had emerged and the boy who said she got hit with the ugly stick was in line to take her out. She agreed and offered to pick him up.

After wrongfully running up a bill at The Whitney, a very exclusive restaurant inside of a mansion, she slipped out and drove away without looking back – leaving him with the bill and without a ride. That was the first of many paybacks but soon she would fall for guy after guy after guy and decided to stop her streak of revenge.

"God, please forgive me for being mean to people. I was wrong but those guys said some hurtful things to me over the years. God, these people keep saying that help is on the way, could you please send Amber? God, these people keep asking me if I'm okay, can't they see that I'm not okay? Can't they see that something is wrong with my face? God, don't let anything be wrong with my face, I need it so bad."

Jade heard sirens in the distance. Then, she heard one last voice before she slowly faded yet again. The voice said that everything begins within.

~

Chapter Eleven

Three weeks had passed and no one from The Ballroom had seen or heard from Jade. Jeff and Brooke were naturally concerned as telephone calls had gone unanswered. After that, they discovered that another personal trainer from Fenton University had taken over Jade's classes. They had even asked Louisa if she heard anything, she hadn't. Ivan on the other hand was miffed. He didn't appreciate Jade not calling him, especially so close to competition. He didn't appreciate Jade not returning his phone calls or answering the door when he came over. He didn't appreciate Jade not being available to practice these past few weeks. She better not make him look like a fool at the competition.

    He had spent most of the past few sessions watching the others practice while he sipped shot after shot of Hennessey. He felt alone but tried not to admit it even to himself. Even Jeff and Brooke ignored him – all wrapped up into each other as if he wasn't there. Jeff was trying to prove that he was the better man. That had to be it, it couldn't have been the fact that Jade was the only reason they were tolerating him. After all, he was Ivan James.

The students were gathering their belongings as the session came to an end. He was finishing his last shot of the night when he saw Jade approaching their table. He headed toward her, ready to give her a piece of his mind for not getting in touch with him after three whole weeks. Meeting her half-way on the dance floor, he stopped short. "Amber!"

"Ivan," she said flatly. Brushing past him, she said, "I'd like to speak to you, Jeff, Brooke and Louisa."

He fell in step behind her as she searched for the others. Irritated by her reaction toward him, he grabbed her by the arm, stopping her.

"Let me go, Ivan," she warned.

He released her. "I haven't done anything to you!"

"You are a jerk Ivan and I'm mad that my sister can't see through you or won't see through you." She continued walking toward the tables where the foursome ordinarily sat and found Jeff and Brooke sharing a moment. She thought what a fool Jade had been to let Jeff get away but from what she'd heard about Brooke, she was deserving of a Jeff and a Jeff of a Brooke. Jade had her own issues she needed to work through.

Brooke looked up and saw her with Ivan close on her heels. "Hi, Amber," she said shaking her hand. "Is Jade all right?"

Amber nodded and then shook Jeff's hand. "I guess. Is Louisa available? I'd like to speak with you all at the same time."

"I'll check," Jeff offered and walked off.

Brooke pulled out a chair. "Sit down, Amber. Can I get you some water, you look a little piqued."

"That would be good," she said sitting down.

"I'll get it," Ivan said out of obligation. It was the least he could do to prove to Amber that he wasn't a jerk, that he was thoughtful and caring, too.

Within moments, Louisa returned just as concerned as the others and Ivan returned with a bottle of water.

Taking a sip of water, Amber told them about Jade's accident and that she had been in the hospital recuperating. Amber told them that Jade was coming along as well as expected and would be ready to compete. In fact, Jade was looking forward to it.

"I'm glad she made it through," Louisa said. "We were all worried something awful about her. We tried calling and I checked my voice mail and e-mail frequently to see if she had contacted me."

"I know," Amber responded. "She sends her apologies, she just wasn't in the position to get to all of you as she would had liked to do."

"We understand," Jeff said sincerely. "How is she feeling?"

"She's actually better than I expected." Amber answered. "She's in good spirits and she can't wait to come back to dance. She misses it so much."

"And we can't wait to have her back," Louisa responded.

"Thank you," Amber said. "Jade gave me your cards and told me to call each of you but I knew I would be able to find you all at The Ballroom and I thought that it would be a great opportunity to tell you all at once."

"We appreciate it," Brooke said. "Thanks for coming by. And as Louisa said, we were all worried about her. Can we see her? Call her? Send her flowers?"

Amber shook her head in confusion. "Well, yes and no. She's at Fenton Medical Center, the downtown facility, and you're more than welcome to send flowers or call but she only wants to see Ivan right now."

It was silent for a moment, everybody letting that revelation settle, everybody choosing their next words, if any, very carefully. Ivan spoke first. "That's good news," he said proudly. "I only want to see her, too. We have so much to talk about since the competition is around the corner."

No one said a word.

"Thank you," he said not sure where else to go.

"Don't thank me," Amber snapped. "Thank Jade when you see her and be sure to ask her how she's feeling." Turning her attention away from him, she said to the others, "I'm sorry."

Brooke wrapped an arm around Amber's shoulder. "No apologies necessary Amber. We're just glad that Jade wasn't killed in the crash. Jeff and I will call her and I'm sure Louisa will, too."

"I will," Louisa responded. "And on behalf of staff and students, The Ballroom will send flowers."

Amber pulled a pad of paper from her purse and scribbled the room number on three pieces of paper.

She passed one to Louisa and two to Brooke. "Jade's room number," she said, finishing her water.

Brooke held back a giggle and passed the other piece of paper to Ivan.

"Thank you," Ivan said softly.

Hearing her name being called in the distance, Louisa said, "Amber, thanks again for stopping by. I will have the flowers sent in the morning. In the meantime, tell Jade I'm very sorry about the accident and I can't wait to see her on this floor for the competition." She pulled Amber in an embrace.

Pulling out of her embrace, Amber promised that she'd give Jade the message.

"Amber," Brooke began. "You look like you've had a long day."

"I did have a long day, like each day since the accident. I spend most of my time with Jade and the other half taking care of her business and mine. One can say that I'm exhausted and could use a half of a minute for a break."

"Good," Brooke responded. "That's just what I wanted to hear because Jeff and I are going to meet Ingrid—"

"I've met Ingrid right, your best friend?"

"Yeah, you met her sometime ago."

"I remember her."

"Well, she's meeting us at Skye's for dessert. Please come with us, we won't take no for an answer."

Amber looked at her watch. "Thanks for offering but it's getting late."

"A great way to end the night," Jeff told her.

She sighed. "All right, you twisted my arm. Besides, I hear the strawberry cheese cake just melts in your mouth," Amber said, cheering up as she rose from her chair.

"Well, here's your chance to see for yourself," Brooke said.

Ivan watched the interaction and frowned. It was almost as if they had forgotten that he was there. They hadn't even asked him to join them. That was fine, he was Ivan James. He didn't need them to invite him anywhere.

Jeff asked Ivan, "Are you coming, too?"

"Nah," Ivan responded, knowing Jeff was only being polite. Besides, Jade was the only important one at the moment. She didn't want to see anybody but him and he would deliver. He hadn't seen that gorgeous face in a while and he missed that. Plus, so much time had passed; it was time to pick up where they'd left off.

~

Chapter Twelve

Fenton Medical Center was quiet for a Sunday morning. The small and private hospital had fewer patients than their other facilities. Ivan, stylish and cocky as usual, breezed through the lobby as if he owned the place. He even stopped to engage in several conversations with different woman before going into the gift shop. He was able to talk the clerk into giving him a dozen long stem yellow roses for half the price. Then he decided to get on the elevator and head to Jade's floor.

Stepping aside to let a lady on first, he got on behind her and struck up a conversation. The woman was visiting a co-worker not a lover. She was admiring the roses so he took one out and gave her the rest, along with his telephone number. He got off first and when the elevators closed behind him, he wondered what she had to offer. Walking down the hall, he slowed his pace. He really hated hospitals and tried not to dwell on it too much.

That was difficult because he absolutely hated hospitals.

Reaching into his pocket, Ivan checked the paper for Jade's room number and made sure that he was heading in the right direction. Ivan smirked to himself as he tossed the paper in a trash can, thinking about how Amber didn't want to give him the room number. She had better get used to him being around because Ivan had finally figured out Jade's worth and there was no way he was letting her go now. Amber had better put her seat belt on and enjoy the ride.

He knocked on Jade's door as he pushed it open. He called out to her but she didn't respond. He called out for her again. This time she responded from the lavatory, asking him for a few minutes. He tossed the rose on the bed and looked around before turning on the television set, flipping the channels.

"I've missed you," he said.

"I've missed you, too," she responded.

"I missed you so much, I bought you a rose," he said.

"A rose? They don't sell them by the dozens anymore?"

He laughed. She didn't. "A single rose sends a loud message?" he said quickly.

"Is it in a vase?"

"No," he said a little impatient.

"Just put it in a vase with the other flowers," she said evenly.

Ivan saw a vase he could have used but did not. He had actually regretted giving the lady those roses. Seeing the flowers all over her room only showed him up, made him look cheap. He even contemplated reading the cards. Ivan had finally discovered her worth, now was not the time for some punk to come interfere with that. He stood in front of the window, glaring out. Deep in his own thoughts, he didn't hear her come up behind him but felt her wrap her arms around his waist. She whispered, "Thanks for coming to see me."

"You really shouldn't scare me," he teased.

"Not trying to scare you," she said still holding onto him. "Just haven't seen you in so long and don't want to let you go."

"You feel good."

"You feel good in my arms."

Ivan turned around and embraced her tightly. "You better get those lips ready," he told her as she pressed her head tightly to his chest.

"Ready," she told him.

Pulling out of the embrace, he held her at arms length. Within seconds, Ivan jumped back, blinked a few times and yelled, "Your face!"

She was literally frozen in place. Jade couldn't move even if she wanted to turn away.

Ivan continued stepping back until the windowsill stopped him. "You didn't tell me about your face!"

"What is there to tell you? I didn't think it was a big deal," she said, now for the first time self-conscious.

"You didn't think it was a big deal?" he yelled.

She looked away embarrassed. "So my face is scarred. I was in an accident remember? Don't you think it's a big deal that I'm alive and the worse that happened was a couple of scars?"

"Permanent scars!"

"The doctors fixed my face as best as possible for now. I'll have another surgery after the competition."

"So you'll be wearing make-up at the competition and that'll cover *those scars!*"

"Maybe, maybe not," she said sheepishly."

Ivan took a deep breath in and let it out. Besides the chatter coming from the television, there was an uncomfortable silence hanging between them. He watched the new Jade walk to her bed and sit down before bowing her head. He realized that the old Jade was gone forever and he was not happy about it.

Jade finally broke the long silence and said, "I can still dance."

"I know," he answered quietly.

More uncomfortable silence.

"When do you want to start practicing?" she asked seeing that he hadn't shut her out.

"Well, that's why I came to see you," he began. "Something came up and I won't be able to be your partner in the competition. I'm glad you survived the crash though and I want to keep in touch." He brushed past her not giving her a second glance. Ivan reached the door and thought he heard a sniffle but wasn't sure. It didn't matter, tears, in fact, emotions of any kind didn't move him. He had been successful in building a wall to protect him from feelings. He was Ivan James. He slammed the door shut behind him.

Out of the hospital within minutes, he sped across town and found himself at I. James Service Center once again. And once again he had no idea why he was there. The service center was empty, not a customer in sight. *Ah ha, business must be going down*, he said to himself. He drove a little closer and saw the service center's lights out and that it was totally empty. *Did Ian close the service center for lack of business? No better for his arrogant tail*, He thought aloud. Letting his car run, he got out and walked up to the front door. Reading the store hours he sighed when he remembered that it was Sunday. He took a moment to read an advertisement in the window. *Coming Soon: I. James Service Center, Northwest Location.* He read it a few times before he heard the telephone ringing from inside the service center. He shook his head, *Ian even gets calls after hours.* He slammed his fist on the window, hopped back in his Corvette and sped off.

Driving without any destination in particular, he found himself on Ian's street. He parked a few houses down, just enough to see Ian's home. He saw a shiny black Jaguar in the driveway and then he saw his nieces, Mallori and Nicole, run out the front door. The girls were beautiful in their purple dresses with hair full of purple and white barrettes and ribbons. They looked exactly like Ian. The girls were laughing and playing on the lawn with their baby dolls in one hand and Bibles just small enough for them to carry in the other. Dionne, his sister-in-law, came out as stylish and as classic as ever. Her hair pinned up and navy blue suit made Dionne look elegant. She calmed the girls down and helped them into the car. Clutching a Bible to her chest and purse in hand, she talked to her daughters while waiting for Ian.

He came out, decked out in his navy blue suit and tie. Walking proudly toward his family, he smiled at them and waved to his girls, who were waving at him through the window as if it were the first time seeing him. He passed his Bible to his wife before helping her into the car. As Ian started for the driver's side, he looked in Ivan's direction. Ivan couldn't look away. He wasn't sure if Ian knew that he was there. It seemed like they stared off for a moment before Ian continued to the driver's side and climbed inside. He drove off in the opposite direction. Ivan's eyes burned but he refused to let go. Could that ever be him? Could that have ever been him – him and Jade?

~

Chapter Thirteen

The snow and ice had finally melted, making way for changing seasons. Nature was busy blossoming in change and ushering in new beginnings – officially spring. The air damp and a little cool most days and rainy the others but still pleasant.

Brooke had packed a picnic basket with Jeff's favorite sandwich and pop and headed to the *Detroit Daily*. She was anxious about surprising him with lunch. Brooke had been content with letting her relationship with Jeff evolve and she was more than ecstatic about the outcome. No pressure. No rush between them, just a walk down easy street.

She tried to determine exactly what it was about Jeff that was so captivating. His drive? His will, motivation and determination? His appeal? Maybe it was the way he looked at her and blushed or that he called her each night at nine o'clock and every morning before her shift. Being with Jeff was new and exciting. It was comforting, passionate and intense. It was sweet, it was secure and it was warm – unlike any other experience.

The surprise lunch with Jeff had fortunately made his day just as much as it made hers. Although a little chilly, they sat on the park bench and talked about nothing. He playfully pinched her chin and promised to visit later that evening so that he could play the saxophone for her. She would count the minutes.

Brooke had finally settled in for the evening as she continued counting the minutes until Jeff's arrival. Jade had crossed her mind several times and decided to call. She left a kind message. Brooke had just sat on the deck and was sipping her favorite cinnamon spice tea when she saw Jade's number appear on her cellular phone. She smiled. "Hey, Jade! How are you feeling?"

"Hey, Brooke. I'm doing okay, I guess," she said sadly. "I got your message. It was so nice to hear your voice and I thank you for calling to see about me."

"Not a problem. You're quite welcome. I had been thinking about you and was wondering how you've been doing. What's up?"

"Nothing much. I'm just recovering at home."

Brooke sipped her tea and wondered about Jade's tone. The always-upbeat girl was truly down in the dumps. "Is there anything you need? Anything I can do? I'd be more than happy to come over if you're up for company."

"No thanks. Everything is everything."

Changing the subject, Brooke said, "Everybody at The Ballroom has been asking about you."

"I received the flowers and plan to get a thank you card in the mail soon. Tell everybody I said hello and that I'm well."

Brooke paused. "What's the matter, Jade?" It was quiet but Brooke let it hang, assuming that she was upset about the accident. Perhaps she could find a way to cheer her up. "What's the matter, Jade?" Brooke finally asked again.

Jade cleared her throat and inhaled. "I won't be competing."

Brooke heard Jade let out a breath and then asked, "Why?"

"It's for the best," Jade had simply responded.

"Amber said that you were fine and that you were going to compete. Did something change?"

"I guess you can say that!"

Not at all surprised by the vague answer, Brooke sensed something strange. Jade loved to dance and had worked so hard for the competition. She, just like everyone else, was looking forward to the competition. "Did something happen with you, with Ivan or both?"

There was silence for a moment. "Brooke?" Jade called softly.

"Yes, Jade, what is it?"

Silence again. "It's nothing. I'm not competing. In fact, I've danced my last dance. I wish I would have never gone to The Ballroom in the first place." She paused and then concluded. "I have to go, I think Amber's coming through the door." Jade didn't wait for a response. She quickly hung up.

Brooke started to redial Jade's number but stopped short when she saw Jeff had arrived with orange roses in one hand and his saxophone in the other. She set her tea cup on the saucer and immediately fell into his embrace. She then offered him a seat and told him about her conversation with Jade.

"Jade dances all the time," Jeff said just as perplexed as Brooke was after she told him the story.

"Tell me about it. I couldn't get a read on her. It's like I've never seen her this way but I sensed that she wanted to tell me something but couldn't quite get it out."

Jeff started setting up his saxophone. "What do you suppose it is? Ivan?"

"More than likely. I got a feeling; call it an instinct, even but he's the only one she wanted to see. His cockiness definitely went to visit Jade and something happened or didn't happen."

"Give her a few days. Maybe she's just down and out about the accident."

"She said that she danced her last dance and that she regretted going to The Ballroom in the first place."

Jeff raised an eyebrow.

"Exactly. That's why I know it's more to it than just being down and out."

"Any request?"

Brooke shook her head. "No. I'm too worried about Jade, aren't you?"

Jeff set his saxophone down. "You know how Jade is. She's very much into herself and may change her mind tomorrow."

"As insensitive as that sounds, you're right but for some reason I get the sense that this is different." Jeff didn't respond. And so noted, Brooke continued, "*The Dance* and *So Amazing*."

"What?"

"*The Dance* by Dave Koz and *So Amazing* by Luther Vandross. Those are my requests."

Jeff smiled and played both of her requests.

"That was beautiful as usual," Brooke said, closing her eyes.

"Thank you, my dear."

Eyes still closed Brooke simply nodded. She still couldn't really get her mind off Jade. She really did feel bad for her. "I have an idea."

"What?"

"Be Jade's partner at the competition."

"What?"

"Be Jade's partner at the competition."

He set his saxophone in the case before he responded. "We don't know why Jade isn't going to compete, maybe a partner isn't her issue."

"Maybe it isn't but let's just say that it is, if you dance with her at the competition, her problem will be over."

"Let's just say that I partner up with her, where does that leave you? You worked just as hard as everybody else. You probably should think this through. Are you really sure you want to give up your spot for Jade?"

"I would," Brooke answered after thinking about it for a while.

Jeff studied her for a moment. "Why, Brooke?"

Brooke shook her head. "I don't know for sure. I guess I'm trying to help her, save her I guess."

"Save her from what? If Jade needs saving, then the only one who can save Jade is Jade."

"I just feel bad for her and I have a strong feeling that Ivan's behind it."

Jeff let the conversation settle and decided, "If that's what you want Brooke. I will find out what's going on with her and if it's a partner she needs, then I'll be her partner. I just hope you don't regret it later and blame me."

Brooke smiled as she stood and headed toward him. Sitting on his lap she kissed him. "Thank you! I won't regret it nor will I blame you, I promise."

~

Chapter Fourteen

While Brooke and Jeff drove to Jade's house uninvited, she couldn't help but wonder if they were making the right decision. Jeff figured that Jade would work out her own problem without his and Brooke's intervention but she insisted that Jade needed a little push. He jokingly told her that if Robby were here, he'd probably call him a lollipop. Brooke told him that at least he was her lollipop. She laughed it off and checked his expression. He just shook his head, then laughed.

Jeff drove in front of Jade's house. He told Brooke that maybe they should have called first but Brooke insisted that they would have to take drastic measures with Jade, especially if it did concern Ivan. She was head over hills for him; the slightest trouble between them would do her in. Jeff had to agree and all things being equal, he thought Jade was a good person and didn't want to see her hurt. He really didn't.

Amber opened the door and let Brooke and Jeff

inside. They all hugged before she invited them to sit in the living room. Amber told them that she was glad that they had come. She and Jade had seen them drive up so Jade locked herself in her room.

"What's going on with Jade?" Brooke asked without hesitation.

Amber let out a breath. "Jade's face is scarred. She has another surgery the day after the competition but chances are, the scars will be permanent."

"Whoa," Jeff exclaimed.

"To say the least. She was fine at first, you know. She'd survived the accident and that was truly something to be grateful for – the fact that she had her life. I went into overtime convincing her that that was more important than some silly scars.

"I had her convinced, too. Even she had to admit that she was blessed to be alive and that each day she would work hard to not let her scars be an issue. You guys know how vain Jade is."

"We do," they said together.

"I know you both could care less about the scars but I knew she would be in trouble with Ivan. The one she insisted on seeing, the one she thought wouldn't care, is the one who hurt her.

"He did indeed go to the hospital on Sunday and decided that the scars were an issue for him."

Jeff said, "Ivan is a–"

"Jerk." Amber finished not really knowing or caring what Jeff was going to say. "I saw that from day one but it doesn't surprise me that Jade was drawn to him because they were both so shallow for different reasons.

"Jade has her issues and I'm sure she's going to iron them out but I do believe that she deserves better than Ivan. She needs something like what you two have."

"I think Jade deserves better, too." Jeff said. "Brooke felt that Ivan had something to do with her not competing."

"Brooke, she wanted to tell you so badly what happened but she couldn't bring herself to do it."

"That's understandable. Jade is big on protecting her image," Brooke said.

Amber stood up. "I'll go and get her. Thanks again for coming."

"Sure," Brooke said amazed at the resemblance between Amber and Jade and even more amazed that Amber actually seemed like the older sibling.

They couldn't hear anything at first but then they heard Amber say, "They know about your face and they don't care. They're here because they're your friends. You should be a friend to them. No, I don't know how you feel having to live with your face like that but don't wear it as a badge."

The grandfather clock seemed to tick and tick and tick before they heard a door open. Brooke and Jeff watched Jade approach with a scarf tied around her head and face. They stood up to meet her and as Brooke reached out to embrace Jade. Jade fell into her arms and cried. "How dare I think anyone would overlook my scars! How dare I even expect it! How dare I think I could dance with a face like this? I'm ugly all over again and no one will ever want to dance with me or be seen with me again."

Brooke led her to the sofa and sat her down, Jeff on the opposite side of Jade. Brooke held her until she had stopped crying. "It's going to be fine, Jade," Brooke told her.

"I really doubt it," she said between sniffing.

Jeff made Jade face him before reaching over, untying her scarf and gently pulling it off. She had begun to cry again. He wiped her tears with his forefinger. Tilting her face, so that her left side was toward him, he rubbed his forefinger over her scar, from the corner of her eye to the base of her jaw. Then, tilting her face so that her right side was toward him, he rubbed his forefinger over her scar from her ear, across her cheekbone. "Help us, help you."

"I don't need help Jeff, I need a new face."

"You're still pretty Jade and I know how much you like to hear that."

"I can count on you to make me feel better," she said sarcastically.

He held the scarf in front of her. "Are you going to wear this the rest of your life because of Ivan? Who is Ivan?"

She took the scarf from him but didn't respond.

"Don't know? I'll tell you. Ivan is a chump and what he thinks and how he views the world has no real value. Ivan himself is insecure so he belittles others to make himself feel superior. Ivan is his own problem, not you. Ivan is immature, self-centered and a—"

"I get it," she said tiredly.

Jeff continued. "No you don't because your eyes wouldn't be red and you wouldn't be hiding. You were going to compete until Ivan saw you and changed his mind."

She wiped her face. "I felt so rejected. Ivan made me feel like no one would want me."

"Who cares about Ivan? Ivan's a fool, lost in his own insecurity. Don't let him win."

"In a matter of seconds, he crushed my spirits more than those bricks breaking that glass."

"Just scars Jade, they may eventually fade."

"Maybe not."

"So! You're still the same fun loving Jade. You'll still be our girl!" Jeff said still trying to convince her.

She let that settle for a moment. "I guess I'm just going to need some time." She paused. "Thanks guys, you've been nothing but good to me and I appreciate the both of you. Are you all set for the competition?"

"No," Brooke answered.

"What?"

"She's not competing!" Jeff said.

"What?"

"We decided you should take her place, if you will."

"Oh no, oh no Jeff, I can't do it and I won't do it. I'm not ready to do it. No, no, no. I appreciate the thought but I'm too messed up by this right now. And I definitely don't want to see Ivan."

Jeff stood to his feet and he extended his hand to Jade. She reluctantly placed her hand in his. He softly squeezed her hand and lifted her to her feet. They two-stepped to music only the two of them could hear as they started moving to the same rhythm.

Placing his hand on the small of her back, he pushed her out and led her into the basic walk before leading her into a few half turns. And back to the basic walk, he twirled her around as she spun on the ball of her foot. They faced each other, he moved them a few paces left, spun her the other way, few paces to the right, and spun her the opposite way. He placed her hand on his shoulder then walked around her while she gracefully turned.

Jeff spun her again, few paces forward. Centering himself behind her, he gently pushed her arms out and in as she rested the back of her head in the groove of his shoulder. Her right leg stretched out and back, left leg stretched out and back. One rhythmic ride of the hips, then the entire movement a few more times. He pulled her hands tightly at her sides. Right leg forward and step, step, step, step, step. He loosened his grip, cha-cha cha step. Gently pushing her waist, she pivoted from left to right to left to right.

His arm sweeping over her head, she faced him again. He pushed her out, raised her arm and he ducked under. Raised her arm again, she ducked under his outstretched arm. Hand and hand, they walked in a circle, cha-cha cha step. Cha-cha cha step, walked in a circle and walked it out. Jeff turned her so that they were back where they started, dancing the two-step.

Jeff stood in front of her, "I'm asking you to be my partner."

He let her go and she sat in the chair, catching her breath taken by Jeff's prance. The perfect contest, the perfect partner, the terrible accident, the ugly scar, the frozen dream.

"Thanks, but no thanks and don't try to convince me because I will not change my mind." She tried to blink back tears, but they fell anyway.

"We don't want you to do something you're not happy with doing, Jade. We just really want you to compete." Brooke said.

Jade didn't respond.

"That's part of the routine Jeff and I've been working on and you could easily learn the rest of it," Brooke said, still hoping that maybe Jade would change her mind.

Jade shook her head. "I hope the two of you win. You look great together and dance well together, too."

Brooke and Jeff exchanged glances. They knew that Jade's mind was made up. Politely, Brooke said, "Well, I guess you can let us out now. Please let us know how you're doing from time to time."

Jade stood up and embraced Brooke, holding on to her tightly before letting her go then she embraced Jeff. Leading them to the door she quietly said, "Goodbye Brooke and Jeff."

They heard the door close softly behind them.

Rain started to fall lightly just as Brooke and Jeff made it to Jeff's car and climbed inside. Brooke sighed but Jeff remained quiet as he drove away from Jade's house. Brooke sighed again hoping that

Jeff would ask her what was wrong so that she could talk about Jade but instead, he made sure the temperature in the car was just right for her and adjusted the air until she said that she was comfortable.

Brooke gave up. She knew that Jeff didn't want to deal with Jade's situation anymore that day. Brooke also knew that when Jeff was "done" with something, he was "done." She was just the same way.

Brooke had tuned into the radio, listening to old school beats from the eighties playing under the "hype man's" announcement about D.J. Tony Tone's old school party at Club Hip Hop. Ten dollars in advance, twenty dollars at the door, ladies free before ten, drink specials, gym shoes, dress up your jeans...

"Jade made her decision," Jeff said getting Brooke's attention.

Brooke didn't say anything. He had opened the door, much to her surprise but she had gotten past it.

"We tried," Jeff continued, "but the rest of this day is going to be about us and us only."

Brooke looked over at Jeff as she heard the "hype man" give Club Hip Hop's address before saying it was just a few blocks away from The Ballroom. It then dawned on her that they were out of the city and in the suburbs. "Where are we going?" she asked him.

He looked over at her and grinned, keeping his eyes on her too long for someone operating a moving vehicle. "You'll see."

Jeff, who made sure that arts & entertainment reporter included him when she went to check out places to write about in the *Detroit Daily*, had been to Arcade Millennium but Brooke had not. However, that hadn't stopped her from taking the game card Jeff had given her, going back to her childhood and playing almost every game. Once they had run out of money on their card, Brooke added more and she camped out on Ms. Pac Man while Jeff camped out on Donkey Kong. They had soon found themselves heading to play air hockey when they met a few "game goers." Brooke started a competitive game of air hockey with the women while Jeff made his way over to the Super Shot with the men.
    Brooke was undefeated and had decided to quit so that she could keep her title. She wasn't sure how well or not Jeff was doing but he was still playing the game so she excused herself to the ladies room. When she returned, she spotted Jeff off to the side talking to a woman. Jeff appeared to have been uncomfortable but the woman seemed to be comfortable – too comfortable.
    She watched them for a while just to see what would happen, if anything. Jeff had been desperately trying to keep his composure while the woman seemed to be going in for the kill. Jeff's back was to Brooke and she moved toward them to unravel the mystery between them. She placed her hand on the small of Jeff's back. When Jeff realized that it was Brooke, he immediately relaxed and pulled her hand inside of his hand. He was holding on so tightly that Brooke wiggled her fingers so that Jeff would loosen his grip. He did.

"Lamarr, this is Brooke. Brooke this is Lamarr," Jeff announced, tightening his hold on Brooke's hand once again.

Brooke extended her free hand to Lamarr who had extended hers and they exchanged pleasantries.

"Would you and Jeff like to join me and my family for dinner?" Lamarr asked Brooke.

Are you serious? Brooke thought of saying but instead, she said, "that's very thoughtful of you but no thanks!"

"Well then," she said with a smile. "I hope to see you both again sometime. Perhaps we can get together and talk."

"Perhaps," Jeff said non-committal. He pulled Brooke along to one of the other restaurants before finally letting go of her hand. While she worked the pain from her fingers, Jeff offered her a chair. Once Jeff was seated she asked, "Who is Lamarr and why was she able to unnerve you?"

"Unnerve me?

"Stop stalling, Jeff. I could have knocked you over with a feather."

"It's not important, Brooke."

"An old girlfriend," it was more of a statement than a question.

The server arrived to take their order. Since both of them had almost lost their appetite, they decided to share an order of nachos.

"Are you over her?" Brooke continued, refusing to let Jeff off the hook. She couldn't explain the reason to herself but she needed to know why Lamarr was able to knock Jeff off his square. She didn't care to know the details of the relationship, just the part about why Jeff was out of sorts.

"I'm over her Brooke and any other woman I've dated but I'm not over you and the last thing I want you to think is that I'm interested in Lamarr."

"You were more concerned about me seeing you talking to Lamarr and thinking that something was going on?" she wanted to be clear.

"You did wonder for a moment that something may have been up with us, right?"

"As much as I hate to admit it, I did."

"Lamarr is nobody in my life but you are and that's all that matters."

Brooke nodded. "Okay," she finally said defeated. She still wasn't satisfied, feeling that Jeff wasn't being totally honest. Perhaps, seeing her just caught him off guard and nothing more and maybe she was looking for something that wasn't there. She guessed only time would tell if Lamarr was the past but in the meantime, she had to take Jeff at his word.

They were quiet up until the server placed the nachos in front of them. Jeff started dishing up the food and broke the silence. "I do owe you an apology," he told her.

"For what?" she asked curiously.

"I just introduced you as Brooke but I could've told her that you were my friend, at least. I made you seem insignificant and God knows you mean a whole lot to me, more than just a friend even."

Brooke blessed the table before she responded. "Jeff, the last thing I'm concerned about is a title, for lack of a better word." Not wanting to admit feeling a little worried when she saw him with

Lamarr, Brooke was truthful when she said, "I know how you feel about me even if you never announce it. The way you treat me, the way you make me feel – that explains it all to me."

They started picking at their food.

"We are dating," Brooke said lightly. "But if and when I become your wife – probably sooner than later – I'd expect you to announce it every chance you get."

Jeff stared at her blankly.

Brooke laughed.

Jeff laughed but only a little.

"I'm kidding, Jeff. You look like you've seen a ghost."

"Stop playing with me, Brooke." They laughed and then started eating their nachos in silence. Jeff pulled his cellular phone out and took a quick look in Brooke's direction. She had an eyebrow raised but he continued to type in a message. Once he finished, he put his cellular phone in his pocket and continued to eat without looking at Brooke.

Feeling her cellular phone vibrate, Brooke took her phone out and read the display, *Message from Sweetheart*. She had Sweetheart in her phone instead of Jeff's name. Brooke looked at Jeff and then read the message, *"Thinking of you."* She blew him a kiss and told him, "I'm always thinking of you." Then they giggled at their silliness before she sent him a text reiterating what she just said.

Once they finished eating, Brooke made sure the bill was taken care of but neither of them was ready for the night to end, they never were so far.

"Where else could we go?" Jeff asked reading her mind. He stood up and pulled out her chair.

Holding on to his hand for balance, Brooke stood up. "Club Hip Hop," she suggested.

"Club Hip Hop?" he questioned as they headed toward the exit. "You really want to go to Club Hip Hop?"

"Yeah, why not? It's something different to do, at least for me. I know *you've* been there before with the *Daily*."

"Am I sensing some envy?" he asked holding her hand as they walked toward his car. "It stopped raining," he commented.

"I admit it, I am a tad bit jealous. The guys who work downtown are always rubbing it in our faces that they get to stop in all the hot spots."

"Working?"

"Yes, checking things out, you know!"

Jeff and Brooke were back on the road and heading to Club Hip Hop. Since Jeff had finally laughed at Brooke being his wife, she thought it would be a good time to discuss how they felt about marriage. They both wanted to get married to the right person one day but surely wanted to take their time getting to the altar. They were both trying to be totally secure – mentally, physically, emotionally, spiritually and financially. And both had wanted to get to certain levels in their careers.

They talked about children. Jeff wanted three, Brooke wanted two but neither cared about the child's gender. They even talked about parenting and agreed on mostly everything concerning the subject. The conversation ended when they arrived at Club Hip Hop but not before they exchanged knowing glances. Between Jeff's media pass and

Brooke's badge, they got the best parking spot and free entry into Club Hip Hop.

The party inside the club was "hyper" than the "hype man" on the radio promised. The dance floor was crowded with dancers; people were wall to wall, some people watching, some mingling, some just grooving to D.J. Tony Tone's old school sounds. He was spinning every song from the 80's and 90's from pop to rap and a little in between: Prince, Culture Club, Michael, Janet, MaDonna, New Edition, Wham, Run DMC, Boogie Down Productions, Beastie Boys, Eric B. and Rakim, Salt 'N Pepa, L.L. Cool J, Kool Moe D, MC Lyte, Queen Latifah, Chub Rock, EPMD, Doug E. Fresh & The Get Fresh Crew – he just kept spinning and spinning and spinning. Ce Ce Peniston, Crystal Waters, Lonnie Gordon.

Brooke stood outside of the restrooms waiting for Jeff to come out when she heard her name called. She looked up only to see Kyle heading her way. When he walked up to her, he reached out to embrace her, Brooke took a step back.

"It's like that!" he said.

"All day long," she responded matter of fact.

"You can't let bygones be bygones?" he snarled.

"Kyle, I wish you'd be gone."

"You–"

"Look, I'm not holding on to anything but I'm not going to act like the air is clear between us."

He sized her up, then stared her up and down, smiling like a Cheshire cat. "Let's clear it tonight," he said lowering, his voice.

Brooke laughed, a little too hard for Kyle.

Kyle grimaced.

She stopped laughing and grew serious. "Boy please! Get some business!"

The two stared at each other. Neither blinked.

"I'm losing my patience," she said calmly just as Jeff walked up. She warmed and wrapped her arms around him, exaggerating the movement, pulling him close, she said, "Sweetheart, this is Kyle."

Jeff extended his hand.

Kyle offered a "fish" handshake and dryly said, "Hi."

Jeff shook his head as Kyle walked away without saying another word. He then pulled Brooke to his chest, changed his voice to sound like a girl and said sarcastically, "Who was that? Why did he unnerve you? I could have knocked you over with a feather. I mean, are you like so over him or what because he's so not over you, is he?"

Brooke laughed and so did Jeff. "You play too much," she said playfully pushing him in the chest. "Kyle is out of order," she said feeling a need to say something on the matter.

"Whatever!" Jeff responded not in the least bit concerned about Kyle.

Brooke stepped out of Jeff's embrace, looped her arm through his as they pushed their way through the crowded club and to the D.J.'s booth. D.J. Tony Tone had set up his next mix before acknowledging them. Louisa had told him all about them and the other girl, he couldn't remember her name. And he revealed that they were his mother's favorite students. He also made sure that his assistant put them on his list before excusing himself to mix a few more songs before returning to them and asking for a request. They practically said together,

The Show by Doug E. Fresh and the Get Fresh Crew. D.J. Tony Tone had been getting that request all night and he promised to play it shortly.

With that, Brooke and Jeff found a tight spot on the dance floor and joined the crowd, taking it back to that era of gym shoes, track suits, door knocker earrings, gold chains and Kangol hats. D.J. Tony Tone did play *The Show*, sending it out to Jeff and Brooke and they danced and danced and danced until he "spinned" his last song.

~

Chapter Fifteen

The Ballroom was crowded with the competitors, judges and spectators on competition day. Not a table, not a chair not any space was available. Brooke made one final round, making sure her parents and grandparents were seated comfortably and close to the dance floor. Since Jeff and Autumn were registering them into the competition, Brooke took the time to find Jeff's parents and ushered them to a table next to her folks. Once everyone assured her that they were fine and ready to see her out on the dance floor, she made her way to the ladies room to ensure that her outfit and hair were in place. Ingrid and Bacari who were just as excited, were both behind her.

In the overly crowded ladies room Bacari refastened Brooke's dress while Ingrid rearranged Brooke's hair.

Thirty minutes before Showtime.

Brooke had to admit she was nervous, but couldn't wait to dance with Jeff. Brooke had momentarily thought about Jade and hoped that she was doing well. It was almost hard to believe that Jade was missing out on this most anticipated day. The day they all had worked so hard for. She would have never guessed that in the beginning they would come to this point only to have it turn out the way it did. She wished Jade the best.

Brooke heard her name being called and looked past the sea of women. To her surprise it was Jade, pushing past the other ladies to get to her. She was clad in a short black strapless dress that flared at the bottom. Her hair covered most of her face, obviously trying to hide the scars. "I can't miss the dance," Jade happily stated.

"Jade?" Brooke asked as she apprehensively embraced her. "What do you mean you can't miss the dance? Did you and Ivan work things out?" she asked knowing that they hadn't.

"No. I just thought a lot about what you and Jeff said, like about not hiding out and getting on with my life and not letting Ivan win. And if the offer still stands, I'd like to compete tonight."

"Hecky no the offer doesn't still stand," Ingrid snapped. "You can't sashay in here just minutes before the competition asking for a spot you were previously offered and turned down."

"I know that it's last minute and I tried calling you earlier today but was unable to reach you. Oh please, Brooke, don't deny me this. I feel I have another chance at getting my life back."

"I don't think that this competition is the answer," Ingrid responded.

"I agree," Bacari commented. "I'm terribly sorry about your accident, really and I'm sincere when I say that I'm glad you made it out alive but this is so last minute and this isn't your answer."

"Maybe not, ladies but it is a start," Jade responded a little agitated. Then she turned her attention directly to Brooke. "What say ye?"

Brooke dejectedly faced Jade slightly feeling obligated since it was her idea. And she was feeling slightly regretful just as Jeff had said she would. Suddenly, Jade seemed selfish. How could she wait until moments before the dance to decide to compete? Now, it didn't seem fair. She decided. "Yeah, of course. Jeff and Autumn are registering us, if you go now, you may be able to catch him and they can change the names."

Jade excitedly embraced Brooke and said, "Thanks Brooke. Oh please, you've got to come with me."

Ingrid said, "You take her dance partner and she has to escort you to him?" She looked at her watch. "Time is running out."

Jade faced Brooke. "You are such a good person and an even better friend."

"Well when are you going to start being such a good person and an even better friend?" Ingrid asked as a matter of fact.

Jade ignored Ingrid's comment and said to Brooke, "I owe you." Jade hurriedly left the ladies room without waiting for a response from Brooke.
She didn't even see the pain in her eyes, nor did she see her choking back tears.

Brooke leaned over the marble sink and lowered her head, Bacari rubbed her back to console her. "I almost said no even though it was my idea," Brooke acknowledged. "I want it as bad as she does. Tell me this is okay for me to do?"

"You're a better woman than I am, Brooksey," Ingrid said.

"She had a chance when you and my brother asked her. Jade will always remember what you've done for her and I'm sure you've helped her more than you or she realize," Bacari stated.

"Are you going to stick around?" Ingrid asked.

"Yeah," Brooke responded. "I can't miss my baby dance."

"Well, I'll stay, too," Ingrid responded.

"I'll tell my folks what happened. I'm sure they'll stay to watch the competition anyway," Brooke said.

"My brother better be happy to have you," Bacari said.

"He'd better," Brooke said smiling for the first time since Jade walked in.

"And he needs to hurry up and make it official," Bacari said quietly.

"I didn't hear you," Brooke said.

"She said that her brother needs to hurry up and make it official," Ingrid answered.

Brooke simply blushed.

The girls pushed pass the women and left the ladies room. Once in the lobby, Ingrid and Bacari went to the bar. Brooke, who just so happened to see Louisa, walked over and told her about what happened with the change in partners. Louisa was surprised and confused but glad that Brooke would stay for the competition.

Someone tapped Brooke's shoulder just as Louisa had walked away. She turned around only to see Ivan. Her sad feelings soon turned to anger. She was now burning inside, hot with disgust. Her eyes narrowed, nostrils flared, jaw line tightened. "What!" She spat out throwing her arms out.

"You must have gotten out on the wrong side of the bed."

She slowly enunciated each word, "What – do – you – want!"

"I was just coming to wish you luck in the competition. You don't have to bite my head off."

"I don't believe in luck and I'm not in the competition thanks to you."

He was taken aback. "You're not in the competition!" he repeated and thought for a moment. "Jade must be dancing in your place."

She folded her arms in front of her.

He swallowed and continued. "Look! That thing with Jade isn't personal."

"I don't have time for this Ivan!" She said shaking her head and walking away. Ivan grabbed her arm, she snatched it back, causing him to lose his balance but he soon regained his composure.

"Don't ever touch me again," she snarled. "Don't even look at me."

"Hey, hey settle down. I don't know who upset you but forget about it."

Brooke bent over into his face, getting as close as she could, practically touching his lips. "I don't like you! You are a simple, mean, moron. You are a heartless, pompous, coward. You are cold, wicked and inconsiderate. I hope you come to your senses one day and stop hurting yourself and others." She stood back and stared at him intently. "And if you say another word to me I'm going to put my fist in your face."

"Yeah right, Brooke! You don't scare me, I'm Ivan James."

Brooke balled her hand into a fist and drew it back.

Ivan flinched.

Brooke saw a familiar face and expression that always kept her out of trouble. Slamming her fist into her hand and letting out a breath she said with frustration, "You always seem to come when the deserving needs to be shown because they don't get it being told."

Winston looped his arm around Brooke's. "I know, call me your guardian angel." Looking at Ivan he said, "this clown's not worth it."

Ivan smoothed out his suit. "I got your clown."

"Look, man," Winston said. "I'm not here for all of this just go on about your business. Believe me, this could get very ugly for you."

"Because she's CIA! ATF! FBI! If she would've hit me, I would've pressed charges."

"Most punks like you do," Winston responded.

"Take the advice," Amber said walking up. "I want to sock you too and you can press charges, it would be worth it."

"Whatever Amber, you don't scare me either," he said walking away.

Amber extended her hand to Winston. "Amber Stone."

Letting go of Brooke's arm, he took Amber's hand in his. "Winston Kelley. I'm Brooke's partner."

"It's nice to meet you but I'm ticked off with you already."

"Why?" he asked, really wanting to know."
"You should've let her deck him, he deserves it."
"Please forgive me," Winston said. "Brooke's my girl. I got to look out for her."

Amber smiled and winked at Winston. "Forgiven."

Brooke smiled at the exchange.

She turned her attention to Brooke. "But you're still in the hot seat."

"I don't even have to ask why."

"How dare Jade ask to dance with Jeff at the last minute. When she told me about coming here tonight, I told her she was wrong and that after all that's happened, she still hadn't learned the lesson. Jade thinks everything's about her and doesn't feel good when it's not. Until she realizes that life doesn't center around her and that she needs to be confident even when the spotlight isn't on her, she'll always be searching for that attention."

"I hear you," Brooke said sincerely. "But what's done is done so are you going to let me off the hook, too?"

"Yeah, Brooke, I'm going to let you off the hook." She said, smiling. "You're a big person with a big heart. My sister should be glad to have a friend like you."

"Thank you. From what I've seen, you're a wonderful sister too. Come on, let's catch the competition," Brooke said.

"Can I sit by Amber?" Winston asked as they headed inside.

Brooke and Amber laughed. "Please do," Amber replied.

Jeff and Autumn stood in line at the registration table, waiting to sign up. While waiting, he told Autumn all about his relationship with Brooke. Jeff told Autumn that he was glad that he ended up with someone like Brooke. It was rewarding to have a beautiful, self-confident woman in his life. He had never met anyone else like her. No one had ever made him feel the way she did because Brooke had offered him something no one else had ever offered before and won his heart. It was just something about her – something magical about her.

Autumn spoke on behalf of both sisters when she told Jeff that they were impressed with Brooke and thought that he had made a good choice. In fact, it was the best choice he had made in a lady. They thought that Brooke was perfect for Jeff. Autumn had asked Jeff if and when was he going to make the relationship official.

Jeff was silent for a moment and was going to respond to his sister when from behind him he heard, "I couldn't miss the dance!" Jeff and Autumn turned to see Jade standing there all smiles.

"What do you mean you couldn't miss the dance?" Autumn asked, obviously displeased and stopping the embrace she was going to give Jeff.

Jade took a deep breath. "Well, I talked to Brooke just moments ago and she agreed that I could compete in her place."

"Just moments ago!" repeated Autumn.

Twenty minutes to Showtime.

Jeff signed them up. He quickly reviewed the routine, the one he had shown her at her house. Jeff filled Jade in on recent changes and where the theatrical steps came in. He didn't have time to wonder why Jade had changed her mind, nor did it occur to him that Brooke may not have been happy about the decision. He was ready to dance and time was running out.

Louisa had come up to the microphone ready to get the competition underway. She welcomed the guests to The Ballroom, introduced the dancers, the D.J. and the judges. She then explained the guidelines, wished the dancers a fun and exciting competition and gave them one final "please remember to smile" warning before clearing the floor and letting the dancers take over.

The music had started. Jeff moved but Jade didn't. He stopped and tried leading her again but Jade was in a trance. He followed her eye contact, it was resting on Brooke. The other dancers took notice and stopped dancing, the music had stopped. Louisa had made her way over to Jeff and Jade, "What's going on?" she asked as the other students moved in closer to hear.

Jade broke her gaze from Brooke and looked at Louisa. "I need to do something. I need to say something."

"Do what? Say what?" Louisa asked.

"Brooke deserves to be here not me and I need to make this right. May I?"

Louisa was deciding what to do.

Jade touched Louisa's arm. "Please Louisa, you have to let me make this right."

Louisa nodded.

Jade went to the D.J.'s booth and picked up the microphone. Turning it on she addressed the crowd. "Good evening," she said swallowing, intensifying the sound through the microphone. She waited for the crowd to respond before continuing. "Excuse me. I'd like to thank Louisa for being such a great and wonderful teacher. Thanks for teaching me the dance and for allowing me this very out of the ordinary opportunity. You see, that's me – always thinking of me but I think I'm beginning to understand what my sister and best friend, Amber, had been telling me all along.

"I met nice people here at The Ballroom, a couple of them, I consider my friends – Brooke and Jeff. I say that now because sometime ago, an accident left my face scarred and I lost all hope but the love and tender care of my friends is the reason why I'm here tonight.

"Brooke agreed not to compete tonight so that I could, after my partner bailed out on me. Problem is, I selfishly decided earlier today to compete and she had no idea I was coming tonight. I wanted to openly thank her and Jeff for their friendship and their kindness. And I want to see Brooke compete tonight, the way it should be."

Turning off the microphone, she headed toward Brooke but stopped short at the applause of the spectators and dancers. She smiled, then gained her composure. Embracing Jeff and then Brooke who was already taking her place on the floor, she mouthed thank you to them and walked off the floor. Jeff and Brooke watched her take the seat Brooke had been sitting in. Jeff watched their family and friends and could see that they were surprised, yet proud of Jade, if nothing else for her courage.

Louisa got the crowd back on track and moved forward with the competition, promising no more interruptions unless an emergency of course. The music started, the couples danced for ten minutes before the judges eliminated half of them. Jeff and Brooke made the first cut. The music continued. The couples danced for another eight minutes, before the judges made another elimination, leaving the final three. Jeff sighed in relief when their names were called. Brooke squeezed his hand, one more round to go.

Louisa called for a short break. Jeff and Brooke took a moment to talk to their family and friends who wished them the best and was hoping that they'd win.

Jeff and Brooke were the last of the three to perform. He looked at his support; she looked at him, never dropping her eyes. For six minutes, they danced with all the passion and energy inside of them until their music faded. They had had fun the entire time but in the end, the judges agreed to award them second place winners. Although they were not first place winners, they were proud of their accomplishment and had enjoyed the dance.

Louisa congratulated the winners, the contestants, thanked the guests for coming and invited everyone to stay until three in the morning.

The dance floor filled up fast but Jeff had stood in place with Brooke in his arms. He pulled back and held her at arms length. He sighed in relief again before speaking. "Sorry we didn't win."

"We won second place at least. I'm too thankful for that and I had a wonderful time. I'm so glad Ingrid talked me into coming to The Ballroom."

"You are amazing."

"Thank you."

"You were really going to let Jade compete in your place?"

"Reluctantly."

Finally it dawned on Jeff. "Well I guess you would reluctantly agree. I didn't realize that and I should have."

"Don't worry, it worked out. Jade's on the road to recovery and look at her," she said directing his attention to Jade dancing with another student. "She's back on the dance floor with her dancing feet in motion."

"I guess our mission was accomplished."

Louisa gently bumped into them. "Either dance or get off of my dance floor." She and Emilio twirled away.

They laughed.

Jeff led her into the basic walk and Brooke said, "Ran into Ivan."

"Yeah? He showed up? What happened?"

Brooke shook her head. "I'm feeling too good right now and I don't want to ruin this moment." They were silent for a while, probably, longer than normal.

Autumn came up to them. "Can I cut in?"

Brooke let Jeff go. "Well of course."

"That's one heck of a woman, twin," she said as Brooke walked away.

"I know," he said confidently.

She stopped Jeff from dancing and stood still. "I see it in your eyes."

"I would really like *us* to be just *us* but what if she doesn't want what I want?"

"Come on, I see the connection between you two. You have nothing to lose and much to gain."

"Worse case scenario?"

"She doesn't want the relationship to change. She wants to date other people, including you."

Louisa bumped into Jeff again. "Either ballroom or get off my floor." She twirled away with her husband.

They laughed.

Autumn pulled her brother close and declared, "Where is Brooke? You need to be talking to her."

Jeff pulled back and kissed his sister softly on the cheek before exiting the dance floor in search of Brooke. Looking throughout The Ballroom, he couldn't find her. Searching a second time, he had almost given up when he saw her heading out the door. He called out to her but she had disappeared outside. Jeff gave chase, praying that he could catch her before she left. And before he lost what little courage he had. He had heard his sister loud and clear. Deep in his heart, he knew that there had never been anyone like Brooke before in his life and there won't be anyone like her afterwards.

It was a windy night, the air a little cool for spring. Jeff had stepped outside, wondering where Brooke had gone. The well-lit parking lot wasn't very helpful; Brooke was nowhere in sight. He thought about finding where she had parked and had started his walk through the lot. He stopped when he heard, "Jeff Ryan!" He smiled and warmed at the very sound of her voice. He turned to her and whispered, "Brooke Carrington."

"What are you doing out here?" she asked, stepping into his opened arms.

"Chasing you," he replied just slightly above a whisper.

"Tag," she giggled.

"You're it!" Still holding on to her, he asked, "You weren't leaving without saying goodbye?"

"Not a chance," she said. "Just needed some air, I guess...felt a little...needed some air."

"Needed some air?"

Brooke noted the sparkle in Jeff's eyes despite the darkened night and her heart began to flutter. "What is it Jeff?"

Jeff said nothing as he searched for the words to say and how to say them.

A breeze hit, causing her curls to fall into her face. "If it's to thank me for that thing with Jade—"

He let her go, stopping her from finishing her sentence. Jeff brushed her hair from her face and gently took her hand in his. "It's not the thanks. It's not the dance. It's the way you make me feel when I'm next to you. The way I feel with only you. I came here for one reason but The Ballroom threw me a surprise - you.

"And now, I can't let you leave until you tell me you're in love with me as much as I am with you."

Brooke closed her eyes momentarily and opened them. She smiled. "You captured my heart in ten minutes and took my breath in one."

"Does that mean you love me as much as I love you?"

Another breeze hit her and he moved in closer to shield her from the chill. She looked into his eyes. "Yes, I do love you very much, probably too much."

He smiled. "That's good to hear because I would like for us to be just us. Is that possible?"

"I'd like that. I'd like for us to be just us, too."

He kissed her and to him, it seemed like he was kissing her for the first time. And he knew that his life would never be the same again.

Beaming over their newfound relationship, the two went back inside The Ballroom and joined the others at the table. Jeff had signaled to his sisters that *their* dream had come true but he really didn't have to do that, they and everyone else could see that there was a special connection. Meanwhile, they took time to introduce Louisa and Emilio to everyone. Then, everyone whether they could dance or not – took to the dance floor leaving Jeff and Brooke alone.

A tall and lean, very attractive woman with freckles approached Jeff and Brooke. They exchanged glances after the woman smiled.

Wondering, they returned the smile as well.

"Officer Carrington!" the woman said.

Brooke wasn't sure who the woman was. She had studied her closely, trying to make a connection but could not. She eyed her from head to foot – then recognized the sandals. And recalled a box with the words "Lady's Satin Sandal" inscribed on it. "Ms. Kent!"

Ms. Kent extended her hand. "Anessa, Anessa Kent."

Brooke took her offered hand inside of hers. "Hi, Anessa. I'm usually never at a loss for words. I don't know what to say?"

"How about you're welcome because I have to thank you. The day you left was the last incident. No one has ever had to come to Copper Street again. Well, except for the movers to come get his stuff out of my house."

"You're welcome and congratulations."

"Thank you. I've been enjoying my life and the new man in my life."

"That's great."

"I'll admit that I am not one hundred percent but I'm getting there bit by bit, day by day."

"All you can do is take it one step at a time." Realizing that they were still holding hands, they let go and giggled. "Ms. Kent, I mean Anessa, you're a very beautiful woman. I could never see that."

"I can imagine." Seeing Jeff for the first time, she asked, "Who is this hunk?"

Jeff and Brooke laughed at the question.

"Where are my manners?" Brooke responded. "This is Jeff, the new man in my life."

She took his extended hand in hers and said, "Nice to meet you Jeff. You guys looked great out there."

"Thanks," he said. "Can you ballroom?"

"I sure can. I heard about the competition and thought I'd stop in and get my feet wet. This is the first time in years I've been on the dance floor and it feels so good. I remember now what I've been missing."

"Well, you have to save a dance for me," Jeff said.

"I will," she said sincerely.

Ms. Kent turned her attention back to Brooke. "You were the most patient, most compassionate and the most kindest of all the lady cops who came to break up the mess I was in. That is why I recognized you when you went up to dance.

"Your face has always been stuck in my head. I'd never forget it. I think your partner's here, too, isn't he?"

Brooke simply nodded.

"I thought so," she said. "Hey, thanks again and for the record, you two should have won first place."

"We know," they said together and laughed.

"How about that dance?" she asked Jeff.

Jeff led Ms. Kent out on the dance floor.

Jade had noticed that Brooke was finally completely alone and made her way over to her. "Brooke, you and Jeff did an excellent job."

"Thank you, Jade."

"And I appreciate you – both of you. I was sincere when I said that I appreciate your friendship and your kindness."

"I know that you were sincere. We're glad to have met you, too, Jade. You are a good person to know."

"Thanks. That's really nice to say."

"And I mean it. I have to ask, what's next for Jade?"

Jade shrugged. "We'll see. I'm going to have to get back with you on that."

"Okay."

She watched her sister and Winston making the dance look terrible and laughed. "Seems like Amber has found a new friend."

"Yeah! What do you think?"

"I don't know. He seems like an all right guy and if Amber says that he's cool then he's cool. Besides, who am I to make that kind of call? You see what kinds of decisions I make in men."

"How long are you going to beat yourself up?"

"We'll see. I'm going to have to get back with you on that."

"Hey, Jade, one day at a time!"

Jade looked in the distance at nothing in particular and repeated Brooke's words, "One day at a time."

"Hey?" Brooke called getting Jade's attention.

Jade faced Brooke and smiled.

"For once I have a feeling that your heart is in the right place and I know that you're going to make it," Brooke assured Jade.

Jade simply smiled.

Brooke's parents and Jeff's parents returned to the table and talked with Jade and Brooke a while before Jade excused herself to the ladies room. Although the day did not center on her, Jade was pleased that she had found the courage and the strength to stand up not only for herself but also for someone else. She felt somewhat empowered and ready to take on the next day. As she was approaching the ladies room she saw a figure that made her freeze in place.

Jade couldn't move and she wanted so badly to be able to do so. Her heart was pounding heavy in her chest and she started feeling dizzy. She had also begun to feel powerless and helpless. She saw that he had smirked at the power he knew he still had over her and she knew that this would be the only chance she had to get things right. No Jeff, no Brooke not even her protector, Amber.

Jade took a step back when Ivan stepped in to hug her. It was all up to her to rely on that inner strength and courage buried somewhere deep inside of her. If she did not, she'd be back at square one and lost under his spell forever.

"Aw, come on, sweetheart," Ivan said as lovingly as he could. "It was all a misunderstanding and you know it. You'll forgive me because you're not the type of person to stay mad - you're too sweet of a person." She hadn't yet responded so he continued. "I'm not sure why you gave up your spot for stuck-up Brooke but that's neither here nor there. I kept my eye on you and you looked great on the floor but I have to admit that I was a little jealous. I wanted to beat the crap out of those guys you were dancing with."

Jade started to brush past Ivan but he used his body to stop her. His scent brought back many memories, as did his style. The closeness was getting next to her and she knew that Ivan knew it.

He moved in closer until their bodies touched. "They say chances are you'll fall in love at The Ballroom. Bet I fell in love with you."

Quietly, she said, "There was a time when I couldn't imagine my life without you Ivan but now I can't imagine having one with you."

"I didn't hear you princess, you said it too softly."

Squaring her shoulders and taking a deep breath Jade repeated what she had said. "There was a time when I couldn't imagine my life without you but now I can't imagine having one with you."

He stepped out of her space. "You will not find another Ivan James anywhere, keep that in mind, *Ms. Stone*."

"That's the best news I've gotten all day."

"Your face –"

"Has turned out to be a blessing thanks to the accident and thanks to you being evil. I have another chance at life but I can't truly say the same about you. You're too far-gone. Thank you for being a creep. Now, move out of my way, *Ivan James*." He didn't budge, so using all the physical strength she could muster, she used her body to push him back. Gaining her composure, Jade went into the ladies room.

Losing his balance, Ivan fell back, colliding with a woman and swearing at her before noticing who she was.

"Such language," the woman said. "It's so not becoming of a gentleman. Oh, but you aren't a gentleman, you're the creep she said you were."

Straightening out his suit he said to Lease Lady, "You're here because!"

"Because I want to make sure that your nightmare gets off to a great start," voice dripping with sarcasm.

"Whatever!" Ivan responded.

Lease Lady motioned behind her and then faced Ivan again. "Here's one of your gullible victims."

Evening Lady approached. "Mr. Hectic Work Schedule. How is that possible when as it turns out, you don't have a job? Mr. We'll Take The Lessons Next Year. How is that possible when you've taken them? *You* can count on cold nights from here on out."

"I'll have you replaced by morning."

"Boy save it. By morning, you're going to have survival on your mind."

"She's right," Miscellaneous Lady said as she approached. She gave Ivan an envelope. "I had sense enough to keep track of all the money I've been giving you and I want every penny of it back." A man walked up beside Miscellaneous Lady. "This guy will be in touch with you on a regular basis to make sure I get it back."

"You can't threaten me," he said throwing the envelope down.

"It's a business agreement," she responded.

Interrupting, Lease Lady said, "Follow me Ivan, there's another gullible victim I'd like you to meet."

Ivan followed Lease Lady out of The Ballroom and across the parking lot. He saw Lease Lady's car parked behind his Corvette. He picked up the pace, passing her and practically running to his car. He saw Sports Car Lady behind the wheel and banged on the window.

She rolled the window down.

"Get out of my car," he yelled.

"My car," she spat out. "Here I am paying for a Corvette that I don't even drive and the one who does drive it only comes by to make sure the bill's paid."

"Get out of my car," he yelled again.

She licked her tongue out at him. "This is a nice car. You know, I could barely keep the note up on my own car, paying for this expensive toy but not anymore. I got rid of the other car so I could drive this one. It's warming up and I can't wait to let the top down on this baby."

"Get—"

She sped off.

Lease Lady drove up. "Well, well, well. How does a dose of your own medicine taste?"

He didn't respond.

"Well, get in knucklehead, it's only going to get worse," she laughed wickedly.

"Get in!"

"Yeah. I'll take you to my home."

"I'll catch a ride."

"With who? From what I've observed tonight, no one in The Ballroom will take you to turn yourself in to the police."

"I have no idea where you're taking me. I'll catch a cab."

"Yeah, right. Ivan James in a cab?"

Knowing that she was right, Ivan walked around to the passenger side of her car and got in, slamming the door behind him.

"Careful with the door," she said sarcastically while driving off.

"Shut up!" he said fuming. They rode in silence. Ivan had to admit that his anger was turning into nervousness. He had no idea what trap she had set for him. Ivan had to admit, he was worried about the outcome. She had just said that things were going to get worse. He certainly hoped that no one was going to harm him. He thought back to the day he let her out of his apartment before Evening Lady had arrived. She had given him a look that chilled him. Had she had something up her sleeve?

What did she know? What was she going to do to him?

Within minutes, they arrived at his apartment complex. She drove into the structure and parked her car where his Corvette was ordinarily parked. They walked inside the building and got on the elevators. Ivan was reaching for his keys.

"You won't be needing them," she said politely. "But you will need a seat belt for this ride." She made the sound of a seat belt locking into place.

Too worried to say anything, Ivan remained quiet. When they reached his apartment, he could hear *It's a Man's World* playing just as it played every morning. He saw Lease Lady push the apartment door open and saw people moving back and forth putting things in boxes.

"Step right up," she told him. "All of your gullible victims would like to see you," she said, trying to contain her laughter. They stood in the living room.

Ivan watched all his dishes from his kitchen being carried out.

Dishes Lady passed him a fork. "Here. I'll leave this for you but everything else belongs to me."

He threw the fork down.

"And here's a can of corn," Grocery Lady said tossing it to Ivan.

He caught it but it slipped out of his hands.

Grocery Lady let out an exaggerated laugh and said, "You'll need it when you get your appetite back."

Ivan watched his appliances being carried away. "I left the detergent in the wash room," Appliance

Lady said as she walked behind the man removing the last appliance she purchased.

"Close your mouth," Clothes Lady said, giving him a Target bag. "They had a great sale and I found a sweat suit and gym shoes in just your size. Everything else is going with me including the suit you're wearing." A man with many tattoos from head to foot walked up. "Well," she said. "Go get changed. Oh, and leave your jewelry on the sink, there's a woman here collecting her belongings and putting them in her jewelry box."

Ivan finally went into the bathroom as he watched his expensive clothes being removed. He returned to the living room and Clothes Lady was waiting with Tattoo man. She snatched the suit out of his hand. "You know this lady," she said as Credit Card Lady stepped up.

"Here are copies of all the credit card statements. I maxed them all out catering to you. And now you're responsible for getting them paid off." She motioned to Tattoo Man. "He'll be in touch to make sure you deliver on your promise."

Ivan was going to sit down when his sofa was moving from under him. He jumped up and watched the rest of his furniture, bed, mirrors, desk, 47" flat-panel LCD high definition television set, being moved out of the apartment. "Got a promotion," Furniture Lady said. "And bought a new house and looked forward to furnishing it with furniture I already have." She sat a stool down.

Lease Lady sat on it.

Furniture Lady kissed him on the lips. "Good night. I'm going to sleep good on these silk sheets."

It's a Man's World started skipping a while before it stopped playing. Ivan didn't have to guess what happened. Electronics Lady gave him a portable CD player with headphones. "You have to buy your own music," she said giving Lease Lady a high five and then left.

Clutching a few telephones under her arm, Telephone Lady approached. "These belong to me. Now, give me my cell phone," she said holding out her hand. "And my BlackBerry," she said, a little louder.

He reached into his pocket and gave her both.

"Thank you." She turned them both off and dropped the cellular and BlackBerry in her purse. "Here's a pick up and go phone," she said passing him the cellular phone. "I'm not doing this out of kindness to you. It's just that I heard there are some creditors, if you will on your tail and they need to be in touch with you." Feeling no remorse for Ivan, she winked at Lease Lady and left.

"Echo, echo, echo," Lease Lady laughed while getting up and closing the door. "That was the last gullible victim." She grew serious for a moment and leaned her back against the door. "Well, one is still here. I was just as gullible as them." She shook her head and continued, "I loved you Ivan and you hurt me and all those other women."

"I didn't ask any of you for anything!" he said quietly.

"How soon we forget. That night when you quickly got rid of me was hurtful. Here I am paying your rent and you didn't even want me around. I came the next morning to beg you to tell me why when I ran into the woman who had been using her credit cards on you and bringing you breakfast from Adorable Dough Café every day. Apparently you stayed out all night and didn't tell her. I tried my other spare key and wouldn't you know the locks were changed. My guess is, since you thought you had all the keys from me and solidified the deal with property management, you didn't leave a net for us to catch you."

"I don't want to hear it!" Ivan yelled as loud as he could.

His yelling shook her for a second but she regained her composure. "I called the leasing office for a new key and of course they were told not to give it to me but you know that's impossible when my name is on the lease and my checks have been clearing. Love struck and goofy as the rest, Property Management Lady came up and let us in. We had breakfast, did a little investigating and devised a plan to cook your goose. We got all the girls together and waited for the perfect opportunity to get our stuff back."

"Are you crazy?" he stated, finally running out of gas.

Lease Lady opened up the door and said firmly, "Get out of my apartment."

Ivan looked at Lease Lady closely. He knew she wasn't playing. He was at the end of the road. He had lost everything. Ivan was going to ask her where was he supposed to go but couldn't do it. The last thing Ivan wanted to feel was alone and empty again but that's just what he felt – alone and empty. Even with a rotation of women, he had felt alone and empty. Ivan took a last look around missing what he had lost. Lifting his chin, he walked pass Lease Lady and left the luxury apartment for the last time. Ivan took the elevator down to the concierge, asking him to call a cab. Where he was going, Ivan hoped that the doors were open.

Ivan couldn't believe what had happened to him over the last few hours. It was surreal in every sense of the word. He woke up this morning on top of the world not knowing that by nighttime, he'd be at the bottom – again. At his lowest point – again. Without nothing – again.

The sound of the cab driver's horn brought him back. He couldn't even get a handle on the fact that he was about to climb into a stinky, smelly, filthy cab in the cotton he was forced to wear and in shoes he had never heard of, let alone had ever seen. He vowed to never be at this point in his life so how did he get here?

"Did you call for a cab?" The cab driver yelled out impatiently.

Ivan slowly walked to the cab. "You don't have to shout," he said sliding into the back.

"Yeah, yeah, yeah," the cab driver responded. Tapping the meter, he said, "Time is money. Now where are you headed?"

Ivan gave the cab driver the address of the man who had carried him most of all his life and had hoped that maybe this man would carry him a little further. He had no other choice, there was no one left. Nothing was really left inside of him, just numbness, absolutely no feeling whatsoever.

He ignored the cab driver's small talk and closed his eyes tightly. The smell of the cab took his mind to a time when he and Ian were children. He let out a breath and started shaking his head, trying to desperately shake off all those awful memories of yesterday. *Just go away, just go away,* he kept telling his mind. You're the reason why I'm so messed up.

There, he'd admitted that he was so messed up but he had tried, really he had. He had tried to do the right thing but for some reason, he couldn't handle it on his own. He always needed somebody to handle things – always had and probably always would. It wasn't his fault though, it really wasn't. It wasn't his fault that he was messed up. Would he always be messed up?

"The meter's ticking," the cab driver said. "We've been in front of this house for ten minutes. I told you ten minutes ago but you've been ignoring me."

Ivan lifted his head. "Okay," he said weakly. Reaching for his leather Coach wallet, he gave the cab driver the last thirty dollars he had. He then removed his driver's license and passed the wallet to the cab driver.

"What's this?" he asked.

Ivan didn't answer. He got out of the cab and willed himself up Ian's walkway. It was late and the house was dark but he had no choice. He needed Ian more than ever before. Reaching the porch, he stared at the light illuminating from the porch light. What was he going to say to his brother?

He raised a finger to ring the doorbell but he thought of his nieces. He guessed they were sleeping at this hour and he didn't want to wake them. A few more hours, the sun would be up, maybe he would just hang around until then. Then he thought he'd just call Ian's cellular phone, maybe that would be less disturbing. As he dialed Ian's number, it dawned on him in that moment that he had put someone else's feelings first.

Ian answered groggily.

"Ian this is Ivan."

"Yes?' he asked, apparently not happy.

"I'm sorry to disturb you and your family at this hour but I didn't have any other place to go." There was silence. Ivan already knew nothing had changed. Ian wasn't cutting him any more slack than he had in the past. Ivan did something he'd thought he'd never do again - ask a question. "Ian, I'm on your front porch. May I please come in and talk to you? I really need you, please!"

"Hold on," Ian said neutrally before hanging up.

Ivan waited and waited and waited on pins and needles. It seemed like it had taken forever for Ian to come to the door. When Ian finally opened the door, he could tell that Ian was surprised at his appearance but probably more concerned about his well being.

"Come in," Ian said as he motioned Ivan inside. Ian locked the door and led Ivan into the sitting room, closing the door behind them.

As soon as Ian turned to address his brother, Ivan grabbed Ian tightly and cried. He cried even harder when he felt Ian's arms around him. He cried so hard for so long, his cries turned into whimpers.

~

Chapter Sixteen

Although the competition was over, Brooke and Jeff had become regulars at The Ballroom. They were there practically every weekend and at Skye's during the week. Still, way over hills in love with each other, the two were dancing the night away as if they didn't have a care in the world. Brooke, who had rarely run out of breath, excused herself to go to the ladies room when someone stopped her.
"Excuse me Ms.," he said.
"Hi," Brooke responded.
He extended his hand. "My name is Ian James. I'm Ivan's brother." Brooke tensed and it didn't go unnoticed. "I assure you that I'm the complete opposite of my brother."
Brooke hesitantly extended her hand. "How do you know me?"
"Jade. Ivan brought her to the center once when they first met and she told me all about the lessons and about you and about Jeff. I had a chance to talk to her the other day between her classes and

she told me where I could probably find the two of you together. She even gave good descriptions – I spotted you instantly."

"What's this about?"

"I'm not sure myself but I would like to talk to you and to Jeff if you don't mind."

She started to answer when Jeff approached. "There you are," he said. Noticing Ian, he politely spoke.

Ian extended his hand. "Ian James."

Jeff shook his hand. "You own the service center with your brother, Ivan."

"No," he said. "I own the service center, Ivan does not." Noting Jeff's perplexed look he continued, "It's a long story. In fact, that's why I'm here to talk to you and Brooke about Ivan. Maybe I'm asking for forgiveness on his behalf, I don't know or maybe–" He paused, collected his thoughts and continued. "Maybe if you know the real Ivan, perhaps you would understand his behavior. Please hear me out."

The threesome sat in a secluded corner at Skye's. Ian sighed before he told his story from the beginning.

Ian and Ivan's mother passed away when Ivan was just eight and Ian was thirteen. Their father, Ian Sr. whom Ivan was the spitting image of, was left to care for them. Although their father worked in a factory, he used half of his money gambling but the other half was used taking care of his boys. For some reasons unknown, Ian Sr. lost his job and things seemed to have gone downhill. Money was scarce as well as clothes and food. And their father turned to women, family friends as they were called, to solve his problems.

Each family friend was aware of the other and each one knew their role. The primary woman stopped by to care for the boys and there was the cook, the cleaner, the launderer, the one who paid all the bills and so on and so on. Still, something seemed to be missing in their father's life. Still out of work and living off family friends, he made sure his boys were properly cared for no matter what happened to him. Ian Sr. kept this lifestyle up until a breakdown would change Ian and Ivan's life forever.

Their father lost his mind – he became manic-depressive. Ian was in his last year in high school. Instead of walking across the stage to receive his diploma, he was riding in the back seat of his Aunt Angel's old raggedy Duster. Ian was holding Ivan's hand and telling him not to cry while their father sat in the passenger's seat seeming to be in a far away land. Aunt Angel drove into the parking lot of an insane asylum.

Ian and Ivan moved into Aunt Angel's in a tiny one-bedroom apartment. She was caring enough to give them her room while she slept on the sofa in the living room. It wasn't much and it was in a deteriorating neighborhood but it was their home. And as rough as the neighborhood was, ringleaders made it clear that no one was to bother Angel James and her nephews. If someone did, the penalty would be harsh. So no one bothered them.

Ian tried to make the best of it but Ivan hated every minute of it. He'd cry a lot and have nightmares but Aunt Angel didn't know what to do.

She was young, single and not feeling very well but she couldn't tell Ian. He and Ivan had been through enough. Instead, Aunt Angel told Ian that he had to find a skill. She told him that he couldn't live like his father had, depending on someone else. She told Ian to find something he liked to do and do it because he would soon be totally responsible for himself and had to take good care of his little brother and that Ian was smart, wise and stronger than any man she'd ever known. Ian wasn't sure what Aunt Angel meant but he went outside, walked around the apartment building and started thinking. He ended up next to Aunt Angel's Duster.

He gently kicked the tires and had begun examining the car; interior, exterior, under the hood, the trunk. He wondered if he could make Aunt Angel's car look and run like new. Running to the old, soon to be out of business auto shop, he talked the owner into giving him all the supplies he needed to repair Aunt Angel's car. It took a few days but the car was almost as good as new. Soon, the neighborhood was hiring Angel's nephew to repair their cars. They'd purchase the parts and give Ian some money for his labor. It wasn't much but it gave him experience and helped him feed Ivan first, Aunt Angel second and then himself, if any was left.

Ian was always the first to wake up in the morning to get everyone else up. He'd make sure breakfast was ready and that Aunt Angel was out the door and headed to the post office on time. Then he'd walk with Ivan to school, try to repair as many cars as he could before walking back up to Ivan's school to walk home with him. He'd make sure Ivan did his homework and had dinner ready for Aunt Angel by the time she came home. He'd talk a while with Ivan then make sure he took his bath and got into bed on time. Each night, he'd say a prayer and console him until Ivan fell asleep.

Aunt Angel had passed away of a cardiac defect. It had been about a year after the boys had come to live with her. Ian came home from a job during lunch and noticed Aunt Angel's car and that was unusual. When he went in, Aunt Angel was fast asleep on the sofa. Aunt Angel must have known she wouldn't be around forever. Ian guessed that's why she told him that he'd have to be totally responsible for himself and Ivan.

Ian had to work even harder now that Aunt Angel was gone but at least she left him what little money she had and her Duster was his. That meant he could do business in other neighborhoods and still take care of his little brother but teach him to take on more responsibility. And the ringleaders were still keeping an eye on them.

Ivan was pretty much unhappy most of the time. Although all the children were poor, he hated being the poorest. Wearing his brother's old tattered clothes and run-over shoes, he hated that he didn't have all the things the other children had and always wished he was someplace else. Ian had tried to comfort him the best he could but he was doing that under a glimmer of hope that things would get better one day.

Ivan loved his brother dearly but he hated his father for leaving them without an explanation and for leaving Aunt Angel and for leaving them without much. He had always blamed his father for the outcome of their lives and if he had been a better father, life would have been much better. Ivan had grown empty and cold to protect himself from feelings but somewhere buried underneath that steel wall was a man who wanted to love and be loved.

Ian had tried to steer Ivan in the right direction but Ivan had decided to do things Ivan's way. In time, Ian had to wipe his hands clean and move forward with his own life. He spoke to his father occasionally but had never asked about the past. However, Ian was sure that if Ivan talked to Ian Sr. –heard his side of the story – asked questions and listened objectively to the answers, then Ivan would be able to resolve any issues and move on with his life as well. He could at least try to get as much information as he could from an aging man with mental problems. Ivan still wasn't ready.

Ian stopped talking long enough to wipe his eyes, catching his tears just in time. "Excuse me," he said. "I worry sick about Ivan and that's crazy. I've got girls to worry about. I know that it is what it is but at times, I feel like I've failed."

Brooke reached across the table and grabbed Ian's hand. Squeezing tightly, she said, "Ian, if you don't mind me saying, you did well for a child yourself and look at you now, owner of not one but two successful service centers. Ivan made his decisions just like you."

He squeezed her hand in return. "I know, Brooke but as much as I hide it from Ivan, it pains me to see him that way."

"We understand, Ian," Jeff said. "We really do."

"Women were taking care of Ivan just like women were taking care of my dad. And the night of the competition, they took everything. I have a feeling something similar happened with my dad. Ivan ended up taking a cab to my home." He shook his head and continued, "I'm letting him live with me and my wife and kids for a while and under some very structured guidelines. I paid those very large debts to those he owed money and hired him as a service advisor at the new service center. I hope it works out."

"Ian. I truly wish you and Ivan all the best. I mean that from my heart," Brooke said still holding his hand.

"Thank you," Ian said. "I know I can't really apologize for Ivan but me carrying Ivan as I always have made me want to talk to you."

"No apologies necessary," Brooke said. "At this point, we want Ivan to deal with Ivan and we want you to keep being strong. You're wonderful, Ian. Ivan is blessed to have a brother so sacrificing and selfless as you."

"Thank you," he said. "Please pray for me and my family."

~

Chapter Seventeen

Brooke had arrived at Jeff's and could immediately tell he had been camped out on his computer, no doubt reading personal and business e-mail messages. She hadn't even gotten through the door good when Jeff had sprung the news on her. The *Chicago Daily* had offered him a job as sports editor, a once in a lifetime opportunity that Jeff thought he probably should take.

She looked at Jeff as if he had told her in a language she couldn't understand. He was expecting to see her just as excited as he was but instead, he saw a far away look, an expression he had never seen before. Moments had passed before he decided to break the silence. "Say something, Brooke."

"If you leave me for Chicago, where would that leave us?"

"Nothing will change between us, Brooke, you know that!"

"But you'd be living miles away."

"In Chicago not Tahiti."

She sat down and put her hand over her heart. "This isn't a joke, Jeff Ryan."

He sat next to her and pulled her hands into his. "I'd thought you'd be happy for me. We always talked about our careers and how we wanted to advance, taking new jobs even if it meant relocating. It's part of advancement and you know that."

"I just got you, Jeff. I don't want to lose you."

"I don't understand why you think you'd be losing me," he said, surprised and concerned about this side of Brooke. He had never seen it before. "We'll talk everyday and I'll come back on the weekends."

She tried to blink back tears now forming in her eyes but the tears fell anyway. "Until you go away and never come back."

"What does that mean?" he asked wiping her face.

"Are you going to take the job?" she asked, gently moving his hands away from her face.

He tensed at the reaction. "I don't know," he said, watching for a response. "But more than likely–"

Freeing her hands from Jeff's grip and standing to her feet, she leaned over and kissed both of his cheeks and said, "Thanks for the dance."

"I'm really trying to understand."

She gave him a once-over before becoming fixated on his teary eyes. "Just know that I'll always love you."

"Brooke!" he called as she started toward the front door. She kept walking until she reached the door. "You're breaking my heart," he said still confused at what had taken place in such a short period of time.

"You're breaking my heart, too," she said closing the door behind her.

Jeff sprang to his feet with every intention of stopping her but he stopped short when he reached the door. He realized that he was too stunned to do anything. He didn't even know what else to say to Brooke, the woman he had fallen in love with at The Ballroom.

Brooke took note of the bright sun sitting high in the sky as she made her way inside the crowded Adorable Dough Café but not even the warmth and brightness of the sun was much help for her sulking mood. Ingrid was already seated and Daryl on his way over to flirt with her like he always did and bring her the usual, hot like she liked it.

"I guess they were right when it was said that chances are you fall in love at The Ballroom," Ingrid said knowing something was wrong but hoping it wasn't something with Jeff.

"I guess," Brooke said dryly.

"What's wrong Brooksey?"

She pushed her plate to the side. "Jeff got a job offer in Chicago and is thinking about taking it."

"And?"

"So he's leaving me."

Ingrid brought her cup of coffee up to her lips and studied her best friend intently. She knew exactly what was going on with Brooke and knew she had to tread lightly. She set her mug down. "Brooksey, what did Jeff say about the relationship if he relocated?"

"He said that nothing would change."

"Don't you believe him?"

Brooke didn't answer.

"Brooke Carrington. Jeff Ryan is all you ever wanted in a man. This is the happiest I've seen you in quite a while. And the two of you are like nothing I've seen. He loves you without a doubt."

"I know, Ingrid," she said softly, clasping her hands in front of her.

"Don't let that part of your life interfere with what you have with Jeff." Ingrid placed her hands inside of Brooke's.

"I already have," she said tightening her grip.

Not being able to get his mind off Brooke, Jeff started to play the encounter over and over again, trying to make sense out of the nonsense. Brooke's behavior was questionable and he was more than determined to get to the bottom of it. He had called her a few times. All of the calls went unanswered plus there were no responses to text and e-mail messages.

He had replayed the last conversation over in his mind. Brooke had said that she had just gotten him and didn't want to lose him and that if he went away, he'd never come back. Why was his relocating such an issue and why was she so sure he wasn't coming back?

Sitting behind his computer, Jeff logged on using his *Detroit Daily* identification and password so that he could access his files. Pondering a moment, he weighed his options and measured the pros and cons. His mind traveled back to the night he met Brooke's parents. Brooke had removed photos from the mantle and placed them in the drawer. *Who was in the photos?* He asked himself. He or she probably held the key, something hidden inside of Brooke. He also recalled mood shifts whenever siblings were mentioned. Finally, he typed in David Carrington, Wayne County prosecutor and waited.

Within minutes, Jeff had all the information he needed and printed it. He must have read the documents five times before Jeff put them down long enough to open the door for his sisters. Jeff had told them about what happened between him and Brooke and how none of it made sense. He also told them about the search he had done on her family and what he had found. While they too were concerned about Brooke, they were even more concerned that Jeff not only found information on Brooke but that he was planning to use it to try to win her back. They had told him that she didn't mention her past for a reason and bringing it up to her would be a big mistake. He'd destroy her trust, push her further away and ruin any future chance of getting her back, therefore proving her statement to be true. If she ever wanted to tell Jeff, it would have to be on her terms.

He knew that Bacari and Autumn were right. The information, however, did explain Brooke's actions. He couldn't help but wonder why Brooke kept something like this from him and if it was still a concern for her, he would have been willing to work through it with her. Did she love him as much as she claimed or had she been making him fall in love for nothing?

When his sisters had left, Jeff gave the information a final read and thought about their warning. He sat behind his computer and read through it again. Sliding his chair over to the shredder, he fed the papers through one at a time. Each shred was like a tear in his heart and the tearing of the memories he had with Brooke. He also shredded the idea that she was coming back.

Sliding the chair back behind the desk, he proofread his acceptance letter to the *Chicago Daily*, made the necessary changes, saved it, attached it to the e-mail and pressed send.

~

Chapter Eighteen

The Mexican customs agent looked at Jade's passport then looked at Jade. "Jade Amber Stone!" he stated.

"Jade Amber Stone," she responded smiling.

He returned the smile, stamped her passport and returned it Jade. "Welcome to Mexico," he said warmly.

"Thank you," she replied, securing her passport in her backpack and heading to baggage pick-up. As a second thought, she laughed at her parents for giving her Amber's name as her middle name and her first name as Amber's middle name. Nonetheless, she was looking forward to her ten-day stay in Cancun, Mexico. Thanks to Jeff, she remembered what he told her about one of the most enchanting places in the world. She truly needed to come to this place to recoup, regain her strength and courage, to rejuvenate and to relax.

The airport bus ride to the Hilton hotel was enjoyable. She took in the sights and sounds, read the marquees advertising all there was to do and see in Cancun. Everything had been smooth as silk, from making the arrangements, to the flight, to her suite, which was more beautiful than she had ever seen. It was the size of two rooms, equipped with a seating area, master bedroom, bathroom with separate tub and shower, double sinks. And the veranda contained patio furniture and a Jacuzzi. Her own private Jacuzzi.

She went out on the veranda and welcomed the hot, arid air and let the sound of the ocean soothe her senses. "They say chances are you'll fall in love at The Ballroom," she yelled. "They're right. I'm falling deep in love with me." She smiled and returned inside. Going into the bathroom, she caught a glimpse of herself in the mirror. She rubbed her finger across the scar on her cheek. She smiled again.

Peeling off her warm, sticky travel clothes, she took a long, cool shower, put on sun block and dressed in her favorite two-piece swimsuit and sarong, and matching beach shoes. Double-checking the contents in her matching beach bag, she made sure she had her iPod, *The Choice* novel, Brooke had highly recommended, her journal and ink pen, sun block, insect repellant, sunglasses, straw hat, pesos, bottled water, beach towel, room key and the post cards and stamps she had previously purchased from the hotel.

Once on the Hilton grounds, Jade breathed in Cancun's scorching air and closed her eyes briefly before opening them again. She started her short walk to the beach and marveled at the gushing sound of the ocean, the sweet chirps from the birds, the exhilarating voices of other visitors, the joyful screams from those playing in the swimming pools and Jacuzzi's.

Removing her beach shoes, Jade stepped to the edge of the beach. Taking her time, she exaggerated each movement of her feet in the sand, pressing them deep and deeper, creating imprints while picking up seashells. She put on her sunglasses and hat, removed her sarong, put it in her beach bag and watched for a moment, sunbathers stretched out on the chaise lounges, swimmers making the ocean their domain, runners taking a jog and walkers taking a stroll. Jade moved closer to the gulf to feel the warmth from the water on her toes. The rushing waves sent the water higher and higher with each wave and she stood still, drawing in as much as she could, feeling at peace on the other side.

Jade spotted an empty chaise lounge under a hut. Situating it just so, she had laid back and flipped through some brochures the concierge gave her to get an idea of some of the activities she might want to do: a boat ride, snorkeling, parasailing, shopping, the night clubs – all of the above.

Putting her brochures away, she looked up at the shadow in front of her. Fernando, the waiter, offered Jade a drink. She agreed to a Strawberry Margarita on the rocks. As he walked away, a couple of guys walked pass and waved. She simply nodded and closed her eyes. She kept them closed until Fernando returned with two Strawberry Margaritas – it was happy hour.

She set one on the table and took a refreshing sip from the other. "Esta bebida que refresca es muy buena. Gracias, Fernando."
"De nada," he replied. "¿Usted habla español?"
"Muy poco. Estudié español en el colegio." She answered.
"Did you study in America?"
"Yes. Fenton University in Michigan."
"Lower peninsula or upper peninsula?"
"Lower."
Fernando held up his hand, palm facing her, thumb extended. "Where?"
Jade smiled at Fernando's visual aid of lower Michigan. She pointed to the lower part of his thumb, "Right there," she said. "In the southeastern part of the state."
Fernando nodded and smiled for a moment. "It was nice talking to you," he finally said. "I will come back to see if you need anything else."
"Thank you. It was good talking to you and I must say, you speak English very well." She paid him in pesos and tipped him in U.S. currency.
"Thank you," he graciously said. "I will come back to check on you."
"I'd appreciate that." As she sipped her drink and listened to her music, she filled out post cards for her parents, Amber, Brooke, Jeff and because of Ian, she made one out to Ivan. She put stamps on them and placed them back in her bag just as it started to drizzle. She had heard that it rarely rained in Cancun and if it did, it was only for a moment. Jade didn't give it a second thought because there wasn't a cloud in the sky. Instead, she sipped her second Margarita and started

journaling her experience, where she'd been, where she was and where she was going.

Suddenly, the sky had darkened moments before it cried. The tears increased and increased until there wasn't another single being outdoors – not one guest, not one staff member. Even the Iguanas found shelter but not Jade, Jade cuddled under the hut and cleansed her soul. It seemed like five minutes had passed when it stopped raining, the sun had come back out, the land dried, guests started coming out again. The staff returned to wipe down tables and chairs. It was as if it hadn't rained at all.

Everything had gone back to normal, at least for a while and the skies started crying again. Still, Jade sat under her hut crying with the clouds, cleansing her soul. She knew she was going to be just fine.

~

Chapter Nineteen

I. **James Service Center – Northwest** was just as busy as the downtown location. Ivan had been busy servicing customer since his six o'clock a.m. shift started. It didn't take him long to get readjusted to the work force, he owed that much to Ian but it did take him a while to adjust to the feel of Dockers. Even he had to laugh at himself for being dressed up with nowhere to go.

A woman, around his age, approached him. She needed her brakes inspected. She'd caught his attention but he willed himself to stay focused. He wasn't quite ready to get involved with any woman just yet. However, her flirting didn't go unnoticed but he succeeded in blocking her out. He remained professional, passed her a work repair order and directed her to the waiting room.

He shook his head and assisted the next customer, a well-dressed, very sophisticated older woman who reminded him of Brooke's grandmother.

In fact, it was her grandmother. He wondered if she recognized him and was tempted to ask about Brooke but decided not to. Instead, he passed her work order for an oil change and directed her to the waiting room. He watched as she walked away. Brooke's grandmother turned around and smiled at Ivan then gave him the thumbs up. He returned the smile and gave her the thumbs up.

By the end of his shift at two o'clock, some of the other service advisors and a few of the mechanics invited him to play pool but he wanted to get home to relax while he waited for Mallori and Nicole to come home from summer camp so he could spend time with them. He went to Ian's office. He had just a few minutes to hug his brother before Ian's clients arrived, they were in route, Ian had told him.

Once out back, he climbed into Ian's SUV and started home. At the entrance of the center, he saw the Corvette he used to drive. The woman behind the wheel pointed and laughed. Some of the former ladies had come to the service center from time to time just to aggravate him but the managers stepped in and handled them professionally. A part of him felt he deserved it, he had hurt so many women but the other part of him felt that if he planted good seeds, good would come to him.

He was usually the first one home so he'd pick up the mail, sort and put it in the sitting room. He came across a card, a beautiful snap shot of turquoise blue wavy water and sand with a clear blue sky. Cancun, Mexico was across the top. It was breathtaking. He flipped the post card over, it read:

"Ivan, greetings from Cancun. I just thought I'd say hello. I hope all is well with you and I wish you the very best in everything. Jade A. Stone."

He caught his breath and read it again and again before going to his room and closing the door. He had taken a moment to think about her, from the day they met and all that they had gone through. He was going to face Jade one day and apologize for hurting her.

Trying to take his mind off of her, he started working on his budget. A budget. It was halfway laughable, he hadn't done that in a long time but it was now of a necessity. He couldn't concentrate though. He kept looking at the post card and thinking about Jade. What if they had been a family like the one Ian had? He probably ruined any chance of that but at least he was trying. There, he said it. It was hard but he was trying. Ian even brought him a Bible and had him worshipping with them. He had to adjust to that but he always felt motivated to live another day and it did strengthen his belief in God.

He had heard their laughter as soon as he heard the door open. Mallori and Nicole were home and he knew within moments he'd hear the pitter patter of little feet running up the stairs while Dionne warned them to stop running. Then, he'd hear little fists pounding on his door. He'd let them in and they'd jump on him as they yelled, "Uncle Ivan, Uncle Ivan." His heart skipped every time he heard it and he loved the sound of it. He loved his nieces.

Ian had made it home by five o'clock and they all went outside for a barbeque. Ivan played catch with the girls while Ian and Dionne busied around the grille stealing glances and snatching kisses. Ian had done a great job with his family, they all seemed so happy, smiling and laughing all the time, always in sync. He was successful in making his daughter's childhood much happier than theirs had been. He wondered how Ian had done it and however he had done it; he'd always admire him for it. Again he thought about him and Jade, what if?

After reading Mallori and Nicole a bedtime story, they fell asleep or at least they pretended to be sleep. He knew the girls stayed up a while talking to each other, just like he and Ian used to do. As he headed to the bedroom, Ian stopped him in the hall. "Ready for tomorrow?"

"I'm ready, bro," he answered.

Ian handed him an envelope.

Studying the shaky handwritten address to Ian he asked, "What's this?"

"A letter from dad." He heard Ivan catch his breath before he continued. "I got it the same day you came to the house."

Ivan handed the letter back to Ian. "What did he say?"

Ian handed the letter back to Ivan. "Read it yourself," he said gently. "The letter only makes a little sense but I think you can use it to start a conversation with him.

Ivan nodded.

"Ivan?"

"What's up?"

"Don't be disappointed if you don't get all you think you need from him."

"I understand," he responded. Going into his bedroom and closing the door, he put the envelope down, picked up Jade's post card and read it again. Someone once told him that chances are you'll fall in love at The Ballroom. He thought about Aunt Angel, Ian, Dionne, Mallori, Nicole and himself. Ivan thought he was beginning to feel what that love was.

Ivan got into Ian's Jaguar, buckled his seat belt and took a breath. He hadn't realized that he had been holding it until Ian backed out of the garage. The next hour of driving was total silence, not a sound, not even the radio. Ian drove into the parking lot of an old building, a building that housed the mentally disturbed, the place where Ian Sr. lived.

Ivan unbuckled his seat belt and got out before Ian turned off the car. He stared unknowingly at the institution and willed himself not to change his mind. He pulled the envelope out of his pocket and took the letter out of it. He read it twice, refolded it and placed it back in the envelope. He waited until he felt Ian's presence next to him before he continued to walk toward recovery.

~

Chapter Twenty

Brooke stood still at the end of the hall on Jeff's floor. She was very afraid of how he would respond when he saw her because it had been some time since they spoke and she knew it was because of her. The way she just "flipped out" with no explanation was wrong but she needed a chance to tell him why. She should have told him what happened in the beginning. She knew Jeff very well. He was inquisitive by nature and a reporter by trade. Brooke was sure Jeff already knew what she had to tell him but she wouldn't let that deter her. He had to hear it from her.

As she started her walk, she could hear faint sounds of music. The closer she drew, the more the sound of Jeff's saxophone became clear.

It Might be You.

She reached his door. Jeff was on his deck, she knew it, playing their song as only he could play it.

It Might be You.

Inserting the key, she nervously turned both locks and pushed the door open. She caught a glimpse of him on the deck just like she knew he would be, putting his heart and soul into the song.

It Might be You.

She stood there for a moment watching him and listening to him play. She almost didn't notice boxes packed and stacked neatly against the walls. This was it and there was absolutely no turning back. She was as ready as she was going to be. She just hoped she hadn't blown it with Jeff.

His sound stopped abruptly and she turned toward the deck, catching and locking her gaze with his. They both stood motionless, expressions neutral. They had so much to say but no words would come out. Someone had to make the first step and Brooke knew it had to be her. She joined him on the deck and placed his key in his hand. "Your parents – your parents said that you can kill them later," she said lightly.

He set the key on the table and stared at her blankly.

Brooke hadn't expected it to be easy. "My calls went unanswered and you wouldn't respond to my text or e-mail messages. I can't blame you. I really needed – I really wanted to talk to you – get things straight."

He started putting his saxophone in the case.

"Jeff," she said getting his attention again. "Jeff Ryan, please just give me a few minutes and then – and then I'll leave."

He pulled out a chair for her. "I'm listening." The first words he had said since she'd arrived had been the driest she'd ever heard from him. He sat in the chair across from her.

She waited a moment before getting up, moving her chair next to his and sat down. She pulled his tense hand inside of hers and waited for him to relax and let her in again. It seemed like forever but when she felt him soften, she breathed easily.

Brooke was born with a twin, a sister, Alyssa. The girls were just as close as Jeff and his sisters and Jade and Amber. They did everything together and since birth, had never been apart. Brooke had taken time to share her fondest memories of her sister and the fact that even if they had a dispute, they'd get over it so fast and go right back to being friends again. They were so in tune with each other, almost as if they were really one person.

Their parents had enrolled them in dance classes as soon as they turned five and they had been studying with the Motor City Dance Company ever since, competing and participating in recitals. They were learning basic steps to ballroom and all other styles of dancing most girls their age wouldn't have thought about. Alyssa's favorite style was modern though, and she wanted to concentrate on that the most.

One year, the Motor City Dance Company invited a select group of dancers to go to Ohio to compete. Alyssa was among them as her expertise and passion for the modern form of dance had paid off. Alyssa had been thrilled about competing and couldn't wait for the road trip. She promised to bring back that trophy to the Motor City Dance Company. Although Brooke was genuinely happy for her sister, she really didn't want her to go. It would have been the first time they were ever apart and she'd miss her way too much, even if it were just for the weekend.

Knowing her twin was upset, Alyssa climbed in the bed with Brooke. She held her hand and talked to her until Brooke fell asleep. Brooke was fine, she just wanted the weekend to be over with so that Alyssa would come back and be with her. The last thing Alyssa said to Brooke before the bus carrying her and the other dancers drove off was, "I love you Brooksey, now and forevermore."

Alyssa made good on her promise. The Motor City Dance Company had won the competition and was bringing home the trophy. However, the bus was involved in an accident on its way back to Michigan. Alyssa was the only passenger who didn't survive. She and Brooke were just eleven years old.

Brooke cleared her throat and wiped her face. "It may sound crazy but I hate it when loved ones go away. I do have a problem with separation but I promise I'm trying to get it under control. I'm sorry." She let go of Jeff's hand and started to stand but she felt his grip hold her in place. He didn't say anything, he simply held her.

~

Chapter Twenty-One

An elegant private room at Skye's complete with a waterfall, balcony with outside seating and a fabulous spread of hot and cold seafood was filled with about thirty guests of the Ryan family, there to bid Jeff farewell. Brooke was at his side, the very place she wanted to be. Also among the guests were Brooke's parents, grandparents and of course Ingrid. Louisa, her husband and Emilio were there, along with Amber and Winston.

Brooke had left Jeff's side just for a moment and took in the scene. Everybody seemed to be in the place they needed to be and Jeff, well, she was more than glad that she still had him and she knew that she would work hard not to lose him again. She was more than sure that he would do the same.

Meanwhile, her parent's seemed to be hitting it off well with Jeff's parents just as she had hoped. She had a feeling that one day the families would be related so they may as well get along - even her grandmother had given her approval. Her grandmother had told her about seeing Ivan at work and he seemed to be doing fine. That made her wonder about Jade. Brooke and Jeff received her post card, which said that she'd fill them in on the latest upon returning to the States. Brooke had to admit that she was looking forward to catching up with Jade.

She took a look back in Jeff's direction. He was already staring at her, begging her through his expression to come join him. Brooke laughed to herself as she headed his way. The assistant business editor, arts & entertainment editor and a columnist at the *Detroit Daily* must have had his back against the wall on some social issue and he needed her to help him bow out gracefully.

Eventually, some of guests parted for the evening or went to The Ballroom, while others went out on the balcony for cocktails or stayed inside to mix and mingle. Brooke and Jeff had finally found time to talk with Bacari, Autumn and Ingrid, much about nothing in particular. All conversation had ceased when a clean-shaven, extremely attractive gentleman in a three-piece suit was walking in their direction. The girls, except Brooke were wondering who he was and was hoping that he was single.

When the gentleman approached, Jeff said, "Robby? What's up man?"

Robby stepped in Jeff's embrace and received his man's hug.

"Robby!" Bacari and Autumn said together.

He hugged them both.

"Oh my," Bacari said in disbelief. "Robby, you look–"

"Good, I know," he said, posing.

"What's with the new look?" Autumn asked really wanting to know. "I'm used to the wild hair and baseball cap pulled so far down you couldn't see your eyes."

"That was the old Robby," he said proudly. "People can change you know." He focused his attention on Brooke. "You'll have to excuse the Ryan family, they're rude people. My name is Robin Storm and you must be Brooke Carrington. I've only heard good things about you."

She extended her hand. "It's a pleasure meeting you Robin. This is my best friend–"

"Ingrid. I know, I've heard about you, too," he said shaking her hand.

"Nice to meet you Robin," she responded.

Still holding on to her hand, he said, "Please call me Robby, everyone else does."

"Robby it is," she said realizing that his hand was still attached to hers. "May I have my hand back Robby?"

"I suppose," he answered, slowly dropping her hand.

Jeff broke up whatever it was going on between Robby and Ingrid, if anything at all. "Robby, what's been up? How have you been? Where have you been? How did you find out about the party? How did you know about Brooke and Ingrid?"

"Let's just say that I'm in the loop. You know Robby finds a way. Anyway, I work for the department of transportation."

"Doing what?" Jeff asked.

"Driving the city bus," he said proudly.

"You got a driver's license?" Jeff, Bacari and Autumn said at the same time.

"Very funny," Robby responded. "Yes I have a license and yes I'm permitted to drive the city bus. Everything I do is legal."

Jeff nodded at his childhood friend.

"When I'm not at work," he continued. "I see a counselor–"

"You're seeing a counselor?" Jeff asked.

Robby nodded. "Yeah. I'm trying to get my head clear and keep it clear."

"I wish you the best," Jeff said sincerely.

"Thanks man but don't even worry about it, I'm good," he said. "And when I'm not only seeing my counselor, I'm dating her."

"What?" Bacari asked.

"I'm dating my counselor. That's right, she couldn't resist all this!" he said motioning with his hand from head to feet.

They laughed at Robby.

"And you Autumn could have had all of this but you blew it. You should have played your hand right," he said jokingly.

Autumn laughed and shook her head. "Thank God I'm no good at cards!"

"You knew I had a crush on you but you always brushed me off."

"You know you were like our brother, the wayward brother but no less our brother."

"Well it's too late now because I'm spoken for."

"I know, you keep reminding me – egghead," she said laughing at his antics.

He turned his attention to Ingrid. "But I'd leave my counselor for you."

They laughed at Robby again.

"Chicago, eh?" Robby said to Jeff.

"Yeah man, Chicago. Come see me sometime."

"Oh you know that but I couldn't let you get out of town without saying goodbye."

"I'm glad you came."

Robby stepped in closer to Jeff. "Thanks man, for everything. You saved me." He embraced him and let him go. "You're welcome and for the record, you saved me, too."

He simply nodded and turned his attention to Bacari, Autumn and Ingrid. "I'm going to say hello to the Ryans, then I'm going to The Ballroom, I want the three of you to come with me and fight over who gets the first dance."

They laughed at Robby again.

"Can you dance?" Bacari asked.

"You know, Robby will find a way."

Bacari, Autumn and Ingrid excused themselves to the ladies room and promised to meet Robby in The Ballroom.

Jeff pulled Robby out of earshot of Brooke. "What happened in Cancun? What about the fine?"

Robby shook his head. "Jeff man, that was yesterday and yesterday is gone, don't even worry about it."

Jeff reluctantly let it go and watched Robby walk over to his parents.

Brooke was checking Jeff's expression. It was curious as Jeff watched the exchange between Robby and his parents. He noticed that Jeff's father had made eye contact with Jeff and winked at him.

Jeff caught Brooke watching him. "I think I got my answer," he said, reading her mind. "I'll have to put the pieces together later but I think my father and Robby had some kind of encounter at some point in time."

"It wouldn't surprise me," Brooke said. "It sounds like Robby is family."

"Robby is family."

Brooke looked around the room before taking advantage of stealing a private moment with Jeff. She looped her arm through his and escorted him out to the foyer overlooking The Ballroom. Directing his attention to the table where they sat the first night they met, she said, "That's where we started."

"Then, I never thought I'd end up here with you like this."

She laughed.

He pulled her close. "What's so funny, Brooke?"

Finding comfort in his embrace she said nothing at first. "It was my dream that we'd end up like this from the moment I saw you."

"I'm glad your dream came true for the both of us. I'm never letting you go." He kissed Brooke and then they turned their attention back to The Ballroom with their hearts beating in unison.

~

When Marquita L. Scott met the Upscale Dance Productions instructors, she knew that she would be in for the time of her life. In a short time, she noted that the professional staff had at least one thing in common – love for the dance and how they put their heart, soul and patience into teaching it.

When signing up for the lessons, her goal was to build upon what she had already learned somewhere else several years before and at the same time make the acquaintance of others interested in ballroom dancing.

Having wanted to be a part of the literary world as an author, Scott welcomed her own idea of introducing characters through a dynamic dance setting. She reasoned that her fun and exciting experience would be an excellent way for Brooke, Jeff, Jade and Ivan to experience the same. She is sure that readers will relate to an urban tale that is true to life, hip, cool and entertaining. And enjoy how relationships are explored in a real and meaningful way.

Scott is a native Detroiter. She has a degree in communications from Wayne State University (WSU). She's a member of the WSU Alumni Association and has been active with the National Association of Black Journalists, Detroit Working Writers, Detroit Black Writers and Women in Communications. Her work includes press releases and articles that have been published in corporate, community and writing organization newsletters. Short stories, "December 16" appeared in *Metropolitan Woman* and "Perfect Old Ordinary Days" was a part of the Talking Walls Project at WSU.

Scott would love to read your thoughts about The Ballroom!

Please send your comments or request additional copies to:

Spread Your Wings Publishing
ATTN: Marquita L. Scott
P.O. Box 19521
Detroit, MI 48219

You can also contact: storytale@msn.com

Printed in the United States
203139BV00001B/1-105/P